BROKEN WOLF

SAVAGE SERIES

MILA YOUNG

CONTENTS

DEDICATION

For those of us who dream of strange worlds and having our own harem of Viking Alphas!

SAVAGE SERIES

Lost Wolf
Broken Wolf
Fated Wolf

Is there such a thing as second chances?

Our mission is simple: track down my mother and find a way to save my sister from the witches. Should be easy, except in our world, nothing ever goes to plan, especially when you're traveling with four sexy, Viking Alphas who are ready to start a war to take ownership of the Savage sector... and me!

The more I spend time with them, the more I feel my mind, body, and soul bending to their wills and desires. This complicates things, especially when my past returns with vengeance.

As if that wasn't bad enough, the dangerously wicked Alphas I've grown close to have been cursed to remain by my side whether they want to or not, making it much harder to trust them.

"Narah, listen to me," Kaira says in a rushed, clipped voice. "You and Jae are in danger out there. Bring her here with us. And whatever you do, never let Mother find you."

My wolf rages within me, begging to steal my sister and forcefully shake some sense into her fighting for dominance.

But I also hate being lied to, especially straight to my face.

My sister should know better, and maybe she does. Maybe that's her intention after all, to make me question her sincerity, because the girl in front of me can't be my sister. This Kaira looks at me with a frozen stare. She's distant and hasn't even hugged me since I found her with the witches. My younger sister used to hug whoever smiled at her back in our town, so something is very wrong with her. And she wants me to bring our youngest sister, Jae, here and put her in danger?

What have they done with my Kaira?

I sweep my gaze across the witches' land, at the amassing crowd, at the High Witch, Lyra. She stands behind my sister like a puppet master, studying me.

Kaira's under the influence of magic, I know she is, and dread bunches up in my chest. She's caught in a spell, just like the cold steel shackle around my neck put there by the witches to suppress my magic. It's the only explanation for her behavior, and I desperately want to snap her out of the haze.

She draws closer, her attempt to appear sorrowful failing. "Sister, please. You did so much to protect us growing up. Now give me the chance to save you." Her hand reaches out toward me, wanting me to take it and come with her.

But my defenses rise.

Ragnar, still holding me, locks his arm around my middle, refusing to let me go.

We shouldn't be here. I feel the magic, the trepidation in my bones. Lyra knew we were coming, she had to know, and unless I get Ragnar and his men out, they'd fight—and die—soon enough. Something in my gut twists and tightens at the idea that they'd die under my watch.

Ragnar came here to stamp his ownership over the land, to sway the witches under his protection, hoping to leverage their power. It really shouldn't surprise me...it's what Alphas do. They fight for territory or women in this broken world, and I hate that females are seen as nothing but objects.

But I'm no fool.

I carry magic, as does Kaira, making us feared by many and wanted by others. Why else would Lyra be so interested in us? She must assume Jae is the same. Maybe by some miracle, Kaira hadn't told her our youngest sister has shown signs of magic. Otherwise, why would they want her too?

I lift my gaze to Ragnar, catching his attention. His face is fierce. He's well versed in the game of negotiations, though even he must know when to cut his losses.

"We need to leave," I say. "Now."

He doesn't protest but gives me a slight nod, which I'll admit surprises me. I expected more of a fight.

"They leave, not you," Lyra barks, green eyes narrowing on me when I turn back to look in her direction.

My heart thumps in my ears because she's crazy if she thinks I'll leave Jae out there alone or deliver her to them. Kaira has been spelled by Lyra, by these witches, so there is nothing to trust about them.

I need to get her out.

I rack my brain and with it comes a solution that I pray works. I lift my head and address the High Witch of the coven with a strong voice. "Ragnar called upon the Lupus Pace, and you corrected him by stating we barged unannounced into your home, making the truce void." I swallow hard as I spin lies on the spot, seeing as I'd never heard of Lupus Pace. But I got the gist when Ragnar invoked it and that it's some sort of protection rite between magic users.

"What are you getting at?" Lyra asks, one of her eyebrows arching, her gaze sharp.

Ragnar's men: Stone, Nikos, and Crius, close in on us, waiting for me to speak.

"That Ragnar's summoning for our immunity stands. I was hauled into your home against my will. I hadn't entered before one of your coven pulled me in, and these men, they are my protectors. They did what they were hired to do and came to my rescue because of your actions." My heart is thundering now, and it takes every inch of strength to not show her how much I tremble on the inside.

"She *was* beyond the entrance," hissed the red-haired witch who dragged me here in the first place.

"Standing in your doorway does not equate to barging in," Ragnar states. "Narah makes a valid argument."

Lyra's lips pinch, while Kaira just watches me like she's not even listening to our conversation. I can't even tell if my sister is aware of what is going on or if she's so heavily spelled that she's waiting for her next command.

I turn my attention to Lyra, holding myself tall. "As such, by the rule of Lupus Pace, we have the right to passage and to leave unharmed."

She strolls toward us, her dark hair seeming to flutter on a breeze that doesn't exist, her violet dress hugging her curves. She pouts her lips and thrusts her full breasts forward. Her gaze is on Ragnar, staring at him, her ruby lips stretching into a smile.

I loathe her even more for the way she looks at him.

"Everything comes at a price," she purrs, her voice sensual and smooth.

A jolt of jealousy spears through me at her attention toward Ragnar, at the way she pauses near him, running her hand across his chest. My insides burn at the sight.

The urge to reach out and shove her away eats at me. Which I know is insane...Ragnar isn't mine, yet my wolf surges forward, wanting me to lunge at her for touching him. The bite mark he gave me flares over my shoulder, stinging.

His arm remains tight around my waist, his body tensing against my side. But he stands solid, not pushing Lyra away either.

Jaw clenched, he shoots her a sharp glare. "I'm listening."

She grins and speaks a few incomprehensive words under her breath.

My skin prickles, and I steel myself for what's coming our way.

The rest of the coven suddenly starts humming, their eyes shut, except for Kaira. She smirks at us, and a dark flash of something savage glints behind her gaze.

"They're spelling us," I say, shoving against Ragnar, needing to get them out. I desperately grab at the metal shackle around my neck, needing it off so I can access my magic.

With a swift electric snap, my back arches, as do the wolves. My chest tightens. I can't breathe, yet something is building within me.

A sense of fear grips me, and I'm tearing at my throat, my lungs desperate for air.

It feels like I'm being squeezed from the inside out. Energy crackles in the air, dancing along my skin, and I'm convulsing violently.

My lungs contract, and I'm suffocating, scratching at the shackle on my neck.

Suddenly, my throat opens, and I'm gasping for it, sucking in as much as possible. Leaning forward, hands on my knees, I draw in deep breaths while my skin crawls. What the heck had they just done to us?

The men are drawing in heaving breaths, coughing and smacking fists into their chests, trying to get more air.

Crius roars and shoves past Ragnar. He reaches Lyra and snatches her by the throat. "What the fuck was that?" he growls.

Her startled eyes widen, but she instantly throws her hand out and touches his brow. Next thing I know,

Crius is flying across the ground like he's nothing but a discarded dead animal. He slams to the ground and rolls a few times before coming to a dead stop.

My heart's thumping at how easily she disposed of him.

He groans and starts pushing himself up. Thank goddess he's not dead.

"You're not the only ones who can bend the rules to suit yourselves," Lyra says, and I hear the smile in her voice before I even turn to be greeted by her lecherous grin.

I really do hate everything about this woman, and each time she glances over at Ragnar, a deeper sense of revulsion comes over me. I feel desperate to do something, like I should be the one to stop her, since I carry magic.

"You can stop all the theatrics now," Ragnar growls. "Speak straight, witch! What did you just do?"

She flicks her hair from her shoulders, seeming rather proud of herself. "You are leaving against my wishes by using the ancient call of protection, but do you think I'm an idiot? What you just felt is a curse I've bestowed upon each of you." She spits the words out, rubbing her neck where Crius had grabbed her.

"Cursed?" I murmur.

"For fuck's sake," Nikos bellows. "What will happen to us?"

My skin pricks at her admission...The bitch cursed us! "For how long?" How the hell do we break it?

"Bring me Jae and I will free you," she explains nonchalantly.

"No," I blurt. "That's not happening. Remove the curse now!" I'm tired of feeling used. It's hard enough living as an outcast with wolves. I don't need a curse from the witches on my ass, too.

"What does the spell do?" Stone asks bitterly, his shoulders curving forward like he's going to lunge at her any second now.

The corners of her mouth curl up. She's loving every moment of our panic.

Crius grabs Ragnar's shoulder, looking pale. "I've got this. Get out of the way."

"No, you don't," Ragnar drawls and pushes him back, shoving a hand against his chest.

Lyra unleashes a sharp cackle. "On our land, our rite is more than words to ensure you don't go against it. Return with Jae before the next full moon, or you'll each suffocate to death at midnight, one at a time, with you, Narah, going last." She meets my gaze. "I want you to watch them die as you remind yourself their deaths are your fault."

I feel sick to my stomach, and I throw myself at her, overcome with blinding-white rage.

Ragnar catches me around the middle and yanks me back, pulling me to his chest. "It's okay, little fox, I know you can rip her throat out, but not now."

Lyra chuckles at his words.

I'm having trouble thinking logically when I just want her to hurt. I'm shaking, tears pricking my eyes at how mad I am.

"Narah," Kaira calls to me, drawing my attention. "Don't be stupid. Bring Jae and save yourself."

But I'm shaking my head, fury digging into me that my own sister isn't on my side, that we so blindly walked into this trap. I should have asked Ragnar more questions, should have done more to dissuade him from trying to make such a bargain with the witches, but everything went to hell after discovering Kaira was here.

"Remove my shackle!" I answer back angrily.

The taste of something metallic on my tongue...magic.

Lyra's whispering something under her breath. She reminds me of a poisonous flower. Beautiful to look at, but her touch is venomous.

The metal around my neck clicks open and tumbles free. It hits the ground with a clunk, and I rub my neck where it pinched my skin.

"I am not the enemy," Lyra says, eyeing the shackle at my feet.

I almost laugh out loud. Does she honestly think I'm that gullible that I'd believe her?

Ragnar starts drawing backward, grabbing me by my arm, his men flanking us, watching for any sudden attacks. "We leave!" he commands.

We've been forced to cower, to retreat, and I strain to hear the words Lyra says to the witches behind her. Just whispered murmurs float on the air. I want to know what she's saying, but we leave quickly.

Our steps are fast as we put distance between us and them. The blow of leaving Kaira is a hard enough shock to hurt. My throat thickens as instinct screams to go back for her and not leave her in the hands of these monsters.

In my mind, all I can picture is Kaira, Jae, and me rushing out of our home in the Storm Wolves pack.

Their fear, their panic, and my promised words that we'll meet by the river. But they never made it, and I won't stop until they are both safe with me again.

"Quickly," Ragnar growls under his breath, pushing me forward to the entrance.

"I can't leave my sister," I protest, pulling from his grip.

Ragnar pivots toward me and takes me by my shoulders, staring me in the eyes. "How are you going to do that when she just stood there and watched us get cursed us without breaking a sweat? They won't harm your sister for now. But we are in danger."

I know he's right. But my entire life I've been looking out for my two sisters. They are all I had left in this world for so long, so leaving Kaira is like leaving a part of myself behind too.

Tears pool in my eyes, but I can't stop them. Not when my chest feels like it's about to crack in half.

"Let's go."

But I'm drowning in fear. How am I supposed to save Kaira before the next full moon in two weeks?

Ragnar's hand is on my elbow and he urges me to move faster.

I lift my gaze to the exit that looms before us.

An overwhelming sense of being watched has me shivering, and the hairs on my arms raise.

I glance over my shoulder. Lyra and Kaira are whispering, and looking our way. A spike of jealousy, anger, and guilt, pulse through me.

What has that witch done to my sister?

2

"That went to shit! And now we're fucking cursed!" Crius growls, brushing right past us, but not before he gives me a look like I'm the one to blame for everything that went so wrong.

For some stupid reason, his reaction affects me, and guilt chews on my mind. I'm still shaking at how brutally bad it went with the witches, my eyes pricking with tears for my sister. "Listen—" I begin, but am cut off by Ragnar.

"Not now." He looks back at the witch's territory. "We need to get as far from here as possible first."

Fine, he has a point I guess. We can talk later.

Crius mumbles to himself, mostly swearing, and storms past us, carving his way through the woods.

The four of us are on his heels, almost running. The hairs on the back of my neck are standing on end with the sensation of a predator sneaking up on us.

Sure, I found my sister, and we didn't die. Those are definitely things to celebrate, except we're all cursed now and are walking time bombs. One of my sisters is still with those psychos, which sucks terribly, while my other sister is back in town with Ragnar's guards.

I keep blinking back the tears that want to rush out now that we're away from there. Part of me wants to run back and just force Kaira to leave with me, to let the witches do whatever in the world they want.

Of course, that's not possible, but try telling that to the guilt slicing through my heart, punishing me for leaving her.

Each time I glance back, Stone and Nikos, who follow behind us, watch me. I'm not sure what they want me to say. But they keep quiet too, carrying the backpacks they'd left outside the witch compound. Stone has his blond hair tucked behind his ears, his light-colored beard in dire need of a trim. Whereas with Nikos, all I can focus on are those intense green eyes with flickers of gold.

What are they really thinking? Do they blame me too?

I feel sick to my stomach with what just happened, and now I find myself in the middle of a tug-o-war between Kaira and the witches, these men, and Jae. I should've been more prepared for a trap, and I hate myself for walking so blindly into that hellish situation.

Ragnar sticks by my side. There was something almost comforting in having him stand by me the entire time we confronted the witches, especially when I felt more alone than I had in a long time.

I keep glancing back, praying Kaira changes her mind and comes to join us, that I was wrong, and she's not being controlled by the witches, but when we finally lose sight of the wooden entryway to their land, I give up on that hope.

Crius pauses ahead of us and turns back in our direction, staring at us ferociously, his arms stiff by his sides, his eyes narrowing. He's standing beneath a huge pine tree, the shadows covering his expression, but I don't need to see his face to know he's still furious.

"This wasn't what I fucking signed up for!" he bellows, coming toward us. His deep blond hair whips over his shoulders. Stubble covers his jaw, while the silver rings at the ends of his beard split into two short braids catch my attention. When the sun hits them, they glint, but I can't deny that even when he's angry, he's ridiculously gorgeous. He towers over me, his muscular chest heaving, but today something wild swims in his eyes, like he's lost himself.

He steps right into Ragnar's space.

The air is ripe with fury, and I step aside, not wanting to be in the center of the fight coming.

"Calm the fuck down," Ragnar barks in response, right in his face. "Plan's changed for now, but the result will remain the same."

Crius is shuddering and not having any part of it. He shoves his palms at Ragnar's chest, but the Alpha doesn't even budge. He's solid, and I'll be lying if I say that isn't impressive.

I stare in disbelief that Crius dared to push Ragnar. I've seen men killed for less back in the Storm Wolves pack.

Nikos and Stone close in, both breathing hard, and a chill settles into my skin at being surrounded by these massive men with the look of war in their eyes.

"Crius." Nikos grinds out his name. "Stand down."

But Ragnar raises a hand for them to pull back, which they do.

"Crius," he growls, his Alpha voice commanding and deep, almost to where my knees wobble in response.

"Pull your fucking shit together. or I'll do it for you."

I can't look away, not when these two powerhouses are facing off, and in all honesty, I don't have the slightest idea what is going on with Crius. Shouldn't Ragnar be the one more pissed off with how bad things turned out?

Instead, an inhumane growl rolls from Crius' throat, his face darkening with fury, and the powdery wolf smell of a transformation stains the air. Crius convulses, losing control. His skin splits down his arms, white fur spilling out, but he doesn't wince. He only snarls louder. His limbs are stretching, his torso lengthening. These Viking Alphas are bigger than any wolf shifter I've ever encountered. Everything about them is monstrous and terrifying.

"Oh hell, he's losing it," Stone barks, and lunges at Crius. "Get him the fuck down."

Ragnar twists away from Crius and comes back around, attacking him from the side. He pounces at the wolf, wrestling him to the ground.

Crius' jaw snaps at Stone who shoves himself practically in his face, while Nikos grabs for his legs.

My heart pounds in my chest and I slowly back away until my heels hit a tree. I've seen enough Alphas fighting growing up to know this is normal...the whole show of dominance, except what the hell set off Crius? Did he want the encounter with the witches to end up in a bloodbath? Is that why he's so mad?

The feral explosion of growls and yelling pierces my ears, while the three of them wrestle an out-of-control wolf.

I can't even tell what's happening with them all wrapped around one another. But the brutal snarls set my teeth on edge.

A white blur suddenly bursts out of the tangled battle. Crius whips back around like the true predator that he is in his wolf form, blood staining his white fur across his neck and front leg. He unleashes a thunderous howl, his head tilting back, the sound ear-piercing.

A shiver races down my spine.

I suddenly no longer feel safe being anywhere near them, and I glance up to see how low the branch is in the tree behind me.

Stone and Nikos throw themselves after Crius, but my attention is on Ragnar, who's stripping out of his clothes. He kicks off his boots and drops his pants. My gaze falls to his firm ass, at the strength in his legs and the muscles shifting across his back. I know I should be worried, and sure I am, but another part of me is turned on.

Just the sight of him naked burns me up, and my skin tightens, my nipples pebble. A whimper rubs the base of my throat in response. My wolf growls for him. She's stirring awake, pushing me to go to his side.

Down, girl. He's in the middle of a freaking fight...not that it makes a difference to my body's reaction.

Ragnar leaps after Crius, his body contorting and shifting mid-lunge. He snaps into his white wolf form, the shift so fast that I'm left in awe. And I've seen my fair share of transformations back in the Storm Wolves pack.

But none of those Alphas compare to Ragnar. Not even close. He is the biggest wolf I've ever laid eyes on.

I'm locked in place, my stomach churning as Ragnar and Crius come together into a brutal clash.

My head hurts because I don't understand what's going on or why Crius got so mad, but I can't get myself to move either.

The pair tumble across the forest floor, Stone and Nikos watching. At first, I assume they stand close to know when to jump in to aid their leader, except they're grinning.

They're freaking loving this.

I've never been a fan of Alphas fighting, but even I can appreciate the sheer strength of two powerful wolves in combat.

Ragnar rolls right on top, his jaw snapping down into Crius' shoulder. Blood gushes from the wound, splashing the earth.

Crius half growls, half whines, his body bucking against the bite. Ragnar snarls, pinning him down, his mouth savagely biting into him.

So much blood.

My pulse is racing.

I wince for Crius. He's been an asshole today, but I don't want him to die.

"Stop!" I scream, unable to control myself.

Which was a mistake. Ragnar looks my way quickly, which is just enough time for Crius to knock him aside with a headbutt. They scramble to their feet, but Crius is already heading my way.

He found me.

I whip around and run for my life, because there is no way Crius is coming to me for a hug. Of course I know the rules...never run from a wolf, but instinct has me bolting. I'm not strong enough to stand still while a monster runs at me with savage intent.

Fear pulses through me, and I race madly through past the trees when a panicked scream spills past my lips.

I glance back at a terrifying sight.

Crius is leaping toward me in great bounds and is practically on me. But Ragnar is right on his tail, with Stone and Nikos closing in from both sides.

Dread clings to me, and now I'm crying out loud as I run for my life from those sharp teeth. And all I can think about is a stupid fairytale my father told me growing up about a girl in a red cloak who was tricked by a wolf in the woods, how she ran from him and still got eaten.

Is this how she felt? Like she might vomit at any moment?

It's funny the things that go through your mind when faced with death. I think of my magic and how that should have been my instinctual response. But apparently, when in a life-threatening situation, my autopilot switches to run.

My foot catches on a root, and I fall forward.

Terror crashes through me as I hit the ground and instinctively curl in on myself, expecting the sharp cut of fangs to rip into me.

An explosion of grunts and shouting bursts from behind me, making me flinch hard.

I crane my head up and look over to Crius being pinned beneath both Stone and Nikos, Ragnar's jaws latched around Crius' neck, growling.

Submission...he's forcing him into submission. I'd seen Father do this to some of his men when he was the Alpha in charge of the Storm Wolves pack.

Sometimes the raw, primal sides of wolves take over and need a reminder they belong to a pack leader and must submit.

I'm shaking and scrambling to my feet.

Nikos is by my side, taking my arm and pulling a twig out of my hair. "You never call to a wolf lost in a frenzy."

Is that what it's called...frenzy? I prefer to think it's losing total fucking control.

"What's wrong with him?" I can't stop watching the way Crius twitches and fights Ragnar. Stone is still holding him down, ready to intervene if needed.

"Crius just needs a small reminder of who his Alpha is. He's always had control issues, you could say."

I blink up at Nikos, at this gorgeous man with thick, chestnut hair running across the top and back of his head with the sides shaved. A tattoo inked down to the nape of his neck. It's of two snakes entwined and biting the tail of the other.

Based on how strong and powerful he looks, and how he speaks so calmly like this is an everyday occurrence, I can't help but wonder how exactly they lived back in Denmark.

Fighting from dusk to dawn? Chewing on rocks? Wrestling with demons?

"He tried to kill me," I remind him.

"We never would have let him hurt you." His words are raw with emotions I can't read.

"Sorry if I don't fully believe that, but I just had my life flash before my eyes back there." My voice trembles. I'm also still reeling from leaving Kaira with the witches, and everything becoming too much.

He steps closer, and for a moment, it feels like he's going to take me in his arms. Is it crazy that I lean forward as if it's exactly what I want too? He pauses inches away, and from this proximity I can smell that sexy masculine scent that is all him. His eyes are wide like he's not too sure what he should do, and when I look into them, all I can think about is the secret he'd shared with me when we encountered the bear in the woods. How he secretly intends to leave Ragnar's pack, worried he'll be thrown out like he has been all his life. Whatever happened to him to make him feel that way is tragic, and it makes me want to find out the truth of his past.

Each one of us is a broken shell, barely keeping it together. Most of my life, I've felt like I have been waiting for something that won't happen because nothing goes well for me. And today is no exception.

I draw my attention away from Nikos and to Crius who is finally settling down under Ragnar's weight and strength.

Crius shudders, and that scent of shifting fills the air. He's changing back, and Ragnar retreats, heaving for breath, watching him with deadly precision.

In moments, Crius is lying on the ground, naked, blood smeared across his chest and neck.

He gasps for breath, and the sight of him breaks me. The skin around the bite mark is swollen, but the blood has already coagulated and stopped seeping out. But he's struggling for air and quivering.

"Crius," I say, stretching a hand out.

Ragnar lifts his head toward Nikos with a sharp stare. Nikos then steps into my view. "You and I need to go for a walk."

He takes my elbow and we move deeper into the woods, away from the trio.

"What are they going to do to him?" I whisper, not wanting my words to carry back to Crius. Looking back, Stone has his back to me, crouching by Crius, as Ragnar sits close, both blocking my view.

"They'll help him. And he needs some privacy, seeing he's got an ego big enough to blot out the sun."

I understand, I guess, and I let Nikos lead me farther away until we pause in a part of the woods where the trees thin out, and the sun beats down on us.

"Do you sense any magic around us?" he asks, glancing at the woodland that is blossoming with plants and flowers. A rabbit hops practically right past us before dashing away.

"Nothing. There are no spells on these woods to harm us. Maybe we're too close to the witch's home," I suggest.

He shrugs, and I move to settle myself on a rock near several trees, resting for the first time today. It's been go-go-go since the morning.

Nikos is a few feet away, his left knee bent and foot propped up on the tree he's leaning against. He's got his head low, and I can't see his face.

Out of the four Alphas, he's been the most mysterious and the one who keeps his distance from me.

Something tickles my hand, and I look to find a black spider crawling up my arm. In a sudden panic, I fling my arm out and squeal, making a sound I regret instantly as Nikos lifts his gaze in my direction.

I flinch back into a recline once more like nothing happened, even though my heart is thumping. I really don't like spiders.

With him staring at me, the first thing that comes to mind spills out. "What's really wrong with Crius? Why was he acting so weirdly with the witches? It almost looked like he had something planned."

Nikos pushes off the tree and strolls in my direction. Dressed in all black, he reminds me of a prowling panther who notices even the smallest detail before striking first.

Reaching me, he stomps on something just inches from my feet. When he pulls his foot back, I find the spider squished to smithereens.

"Crius agreed to this mission for his own purpose, and things didn't go to plan. So he's pissed."

"What's his mission?" I lean forward. "And he has magic too, doesn't he? Just like Stone."

"That he does. It's very specific." He stuffs his hands into his pockets and glances down at me.

"Why does it feel like I have to drag every word out of you about him? Shouldn't I know who I'm dealing with if we are stuck together for the next two weeks?"

"Tell me something." He crouches down in front of me so we're at eye level. And it's only now that I notice the streak of blood along his jawline. "Did you enjoy seeing Crius losing control? How we had to keep fighting him to keep him from hurting himself and you?"

My shoulders rear back. "What is that supposed to mean? Of course, I didn't."

"But how did it make you feel?" he presses.

"Worried about him. Uncomfortable to see him that way." Just as uneasy as Nikos is making me feel now.

"There you have it. That's how he'd feel with us talking about him." He gets to his feet, his face expressionless, but there's a coldness behind his words. "His story is not mine to tell. I won't take that away from him. But, fair warning, it may be something you won't want to hear, so I suggest leaving it alone."

He turns and strolls back to his tree.

I should have been relieved that he gave me an out to forget about Crius, just like I should do with all of these Alphas. Even Ragnar. Except, I'm already on my feet, following him, and my words are pouring out. "Maybe the reason I ask is because I care. Because if I know someone well enough, I can help them."

He twists back around toward me, and I feel the power he radiates. He may be Ragnar's Second, but Nikos is every inch a powerful Alpha too. He reaches over and gently takes a loose strand of my hair caught in my eyelashes and tucks it behind my ear. The way his gaze dips to my lips distracts me, makes me forget what I'd been saying. A ghost of a smile plays on his lips— everything about him always takes me off guard and draws me to him.

I'm an Omega. He's an Alpha.

In our world, men like him fight to the death to own women like me, and I don't miss the way he stares at me. The way they all stare at me, along with knowing they struggle to hold back their raw, primal instincts. Top Alphas like Ragnar reign over other Alphas, Betas, and Omegas. All Alphas in a pack don't stray from the top of the hierarchy, and are ranked in order of Second, Third, and so forth. It's how it was set up in the Storm Wolves too. How I see Ragnar run his pack.

Betas are the warriors, the work dogs of packs. The Omegas like me are the ones who usually carry no power and are used as breeders. Our heat controls us, draws us to Alphas, except because of the magic in my veins, my heat has never really come out completely.

My attraction to Martell, my fated mate who tried to kill me, was instantaneous, but unlike other girls, I haven't fully come into my heat. Mother told me it was a blessing for us hybrids. No heat meant we had greater control and didn't send men into a craze to claim us.

"I'd think you learned plenty about all of us during the bear attacks." He leans forward and takes another lock of my hair, bringing it to his nose and inhales deeply.

His words have me straightening, and I push his hand away from me. "You hate the fact that you shared something about your past with me? I won't judge you for what you said."

He inches closer. Our bodies touch now, and my breath catches in my throat. "Narah, you have no idea what you've agreed to when it comes to making a deal with Ragnar and all of us. And I'm not trying to scare you."

I swallow hard. "What do you mean?" I desperately want to know what he's talking about. "We all had shitty upbringings, trust me, I understand. Try being an Omega in this broken world where females are commodities, let alone one with powers that can get me killed. Wolves hate witches."

He stares at me like somehow he can do one better. "Everything can get us killed in this world. You might have a target painted on your back, but you had parents who loved you. Mine sold me as soon as they could. So it seems both of us may be no better than commodities, but it doesn't change the fact that, with us, you and your sisters are in more danger than you realize." His voice grows bitter.

The ache in his words messes me up. I knew these guys were just as ruined as me, but what in the world is he talking about? I want to tell him that we're in this together for now, but my chance is stolen by approaching footsteps.

I raise my gaze to three figures emerging from the woods, the men returning, and if I wasn't unsettled before, now I'm scared.

What the hell was Nikos talking about? Of course, now my mind is running rampant with worse-case scenarios.

3

RAGNAR

I march into a clearing in the woods and find Narah standing several feet away, close to Nikos, both of them looking at me as if startled. For a moment, it almost feels like I've caught them kissing.

I made the point of telling my three men that we share everything... including Omegas. But seeing Nikos and Narah almost pressed together ignites a searing flame in my chest. She's mine... all mine, and I need her to know this and to understand that the mark I've given her will keep the agony for her rejected fated mate at bay... for now. But the payment for freeing her means she's mine.

I lost my fated mate, too, and accepted that long ago. I'll be drawn to Omegas in heat, but none will lock in with my wolf. It's how our kind works. You have a chance to find your perfect partner, and for the rest of us suckers who never do, or lose them, well, we love with half a heart.

Maybe it's the fact we are both broken that I'm so drawn to her.

Nikos backs away at my approach, and I grab hold of Narah's shoulders, her lips swollen like she's been kissed.

A gasp rolls from her throat, and I soften my grip, well aware that I sometimes forget my own strength. Or the aggression with which I take what I want.

"Are you hurt?" I study her beautiful face for injuries from Crius' chase—her porcelain skin, her long slender neck, her large, vulnerable eyes.

I draw in a deep breath, filling my nostrils with the smell of her sex. It's intoxicating, lingering below the surface of her natural sweetness.

I will never understand how her fated mate could have rejected a woman as perfect as her. But if I ever cross paths with him, I'll destroy him for hurting her.

"I'm fine," she says and pulls away from me, her gaze shifting to Crius, who stands at the far edge of the small clearing, arms folded across his chest, shadows darkening beneath his eyes.

"He won't hurt you," I reassure her.

"Sorry if I scared you," he croaks, sounding almost reluctant to apologize.

Though, I'm impressed by his attempt. Most of the time, he doesn't give a fuck.

"I'm not afraid of you," she says calmly.

She's utterly adorable at how strong she holds herself when it had been obvious she was terrified when he chased her.

"Things didn't go to plan, and we didn't walk out of there with the witches' alliance," I address the group, since we are all together and no one is trying to kill anyone for a change. I don't bring up the fact that Kaira turning up with the witches was a massive wrench in our plans.

"You could say that." Crius' voice darkens, and he raises his chin defiantly. I feel for him, but he needs to pull himself together. As much as he's pissed that he never got this big chance for his grand spell, personally, I'm glad it never happened.

I've been conflicted about permitting him to carry through with his intended spell to overtake the witches from the beginning. The risk to himself was too high.

I've lost enough people in my life and I sure as fuck can't lose him too. What he doesn't realize is that regardless of how that went down with the witches, I had a contingency plan to stop him with Stone's help. But the witches' curse and Narah's sister came in just as handy as a distraction.

I clear my throat. "The witches want Narah and Jae, so we're going to use that to our advantage."

"I vote for burning the coven down." Stone spits the words, his chest sticking out, and Crius gives him an approving nod. "That will nullify the curse."

"Our priority is to find my mother," Narah interrupts, drawing all our attention.

"Your sister warned you to stay away from her," Nikos adds. "Are you sure that's the right decision?"

Except, her suggestion makes sense. "They fear your mother for a reason," I say out loud.

Narah's nodding. "She could offer us a way to get my sister back and to overthrow the coven." There is eagerness in her words, and it has everything to do with her needing to find her mother. Narah had told me her mother carried magic too and that both her parents were dead, so her decision to track her down now shouldn't come as a surprise.

"Or we could be walking into a trap and your sister lied," Crius groans. "No insult intended, Narah, but your sister was a fucking bitch and didn't look too happy to see you. So what if she knows that's exactly what you'll do by mentioning your mom?"

Narah stiffens, her shoulders rising. "And what do you suggest?" she snaps, her eyes narrowing on Crius. "That you kill the witches, if they don't get you first? And then what? Every freaking Alpha outside these woods will rampage to claim the land, including taking all of you down. As much as you hate witches, they are the necessary evil that is keeping a sense of harmony over the land. And I won't let you endanger my sister." She stands tall and adamant, her stance clear. She'll do anything to protect her sister, even turn on us.

"I never said we'd kill your sister," he counters.

She's a smart girl, but too easily led by her emotions. Though, it's not too often I see Omegas with such tenacity and bravery. I find it brutally beautiful.

Crius has his hands now in the pockets of his pants, nonchalantly lifting his chin toward Narah. "I don't want you to think I hate all witches. I like you. But I sure as fuck am not going to die by a witch's curse, either. I'll go down as a warrior."

"It's getting really hard to tell," she answers and lowers her gaze. "Your wolf seemed inclined to want to take a chunk out of me."

Tension thickens the air, and I get it. The mission failed miserably. We're cursed, and everyone wants a solution. But as they say in ancient books, *Rome wasn't built in a day*. If this was easy, the witches would have been in alliance with another pack already. So as far as I'm concerned, this is an opportunity.

"We have two weeks," I say, to break the stretching silence. "So, we'll make finding Narah's mother a priority."

Narah's mouth falls open. "Curses can't be removed, you know that? Unless we kill the witch who spelled us."

I nod. "Yet magic can be manipulated to extend the time. I've seen it done back in Denmark. And I didn't come all the way to Romania to fail. That's not even a possibility I will entertain."

She shrugs like she's not sure she believes me. But I intend to prove her wrong, along with my father.

"You're worthless," my father barks. "A waste of my seed, of my time." The man is large and ruthless, destroying everyone in his path. It surprises me he hasn't strangled me in my sleep yet.

Still, his words are punches to the gut, even if I've heard them before. Too often for my liking, and as much as I fucking loath the cold-hearted prick, I can tell his mood by his insults. The day he doesn't curse me is the day I'll end up on a burning boat pushed out into the sea.

"How was the trip?" I sneer and look over to Mother, who sits at the table pretending to eat and is cutting up the sausage on her plate into dozens of pieces. For her, I keep the peace. For her, I try not to antagonize him. When the bastard is furious, it's her who deals with the fury he lashes out.

He pushes up from his seat at the end of the grand dining table, dropping his fork to the plate, which lands with a loud clunk. "Since when do you care about diplomatic matters? Don't waste my time pretending, son. It's not becoming of you."

A growl rumbles in my chest at his hatred.

"Frode," Mother says, her mouth tight. "Please, just sit. Can we eat one meal as a family in peace?"

Father doesn't respond, but heaves heavily, then sits back down with a huff.

"You blame me for Hel," I say, my hands gripping the back of an empty chair at the table. "Then give me the men from your pack to rescue her, to wet the land with the blood from every last Balor wolf. I will claim his land for me... for us."

"No!" Father roars, slamming his fist on the table. The plates and food jump and Mother flinches. "You will fail, and that you stand there and demand war on them tells me you will never be ready to become Alpha. You think with your wolf, not your brain." He growls, the sound reverberating through the room. "Negotiations are set, and in exchange for Hel, The Balor Alpha's son, Nikos, arrives on the morrow. You will be responsible for him. If he dies, Hel's death at the hands of our enemy will rest on your shoulders."

I clench my teeth and shove those memories aside, hating Father with every fiber of my being.

"Grab your stuff, let's move," I order my pack and Narah.

"And our backup plan," Stone adds, causing me to pause as I turn toward the woods. "We destroy the witches?"

"Fuck yes." Crius pumps his fist in the air. "After we get Kaira out, of course."

Narah's eyes grow stormy. She may not like it, but nothing comes out of being nice in this world.

You survive using claws and teeth, with spilling blood. And if you don't, then your blood will be the one to spill.

No one responds, and frustration pinches along my shoulder blades. "Let's go."

Narah turns and walks into the woods. We march after her. I'd fought my entire life, been tortured, told I'll amount to nothing, so my mission to take over the Savage Sector in Romania will be my legacy to prove them all wrong. Then rescuing Hel and having her live in my pack will be the ultimate way I tell my father to go fuck himself.

The woods darken the farther we travel.

After hours of endless walking, there's no trace of magic, not even a trickle in the air. No attacking trees or losing control of our wolves... nothing. About damn time.

The moon hangs heavy tonight. I want to get out of these fucking woods desperately. It feels like I'm constantly being watched. Like there isn't enough oxygen to draw into my lungs, and like I'm being squeezed into a box two sizes too small for me.

"This is a good spot," Nikos says and dumps the backpacks he's been carrying on a flat section of land devoid of trees. The firs that surround us are still like statues. There's no breeze tonight, only the deathly silence of a haunted forest.

We all move on autopilot to set up camp. No sign of animals in this area either, nothing to hunt, so we'll make do with the dried meat, bread, and fruit in our bags.

"Is it just me, or does it feel like everything is frozen in time? I'd kill for a breeze on my face," Nikos murmurs.

"This place sucks," Stone remarks as he digs through a backpack and comes out with a lighter. He drops to his knees in front of the pile of twigs and sets them alight.

"We've been in the worst situations," I tell them.

"Really? Like when?" Crius asks.

"Like being ambushed in Poland by those female warriors."

Stone bursts out laughing, the sound abrupt and echoing around us. It's refreshing to hear laughter instead of sighs and groans. "I'm not sure if I was more worried about them killing or fucking us. Some of them were bigger than me, man. Though, I still think they wanted us as hostages so we could become their breeders. Not a bad way to go, all things considered. But not sure if that's comparable to this mission."

"Didn't stop Nikos from trying," Crius remarks as he dumps more branches near the blazing fire. "It's what got us in trouble in the first place."

Nikos chuckles and shrugs. "When you see an Omega wandering in the woods with no clothes and calling for help, what would you do?"

"Help her, not fuck her," Stone says and laughs.

"Narah, you've been quiet." I turn around to bring her into the conversation. She's kept to herself for most of the trip.

Except she's not behind me.

Frantically, I look around to find her gone.

Panic races down my spine.

"Where the fuck is Narah?"

4

Today was brutal.

I barely keep it together each time I think of Kaira. There is no way in this hellish world that my sister would behave like she had. It's not in her nature, and the farther we distance ourselves from the coven, the more my chest tightens at the thought that I've left her behind. Of course, I tell myself they won't harm her until we return, but what if the spell damages her?

What if, by the time we return, the sister I once knew and loved no longer exists, is too destroyed to ever be herself again? Magic can have horrendous repercussions on those under its influence, and for all I know, she's been under a spell the past two months since we escaped the Storm Wolves pack.

Mother once told me that an untreated spell can spread like cancer, and the longer they are afflicted, the harder it will be for them to ever fully be themselves again.

They'll be broken on the inside, she'd said. *Much like our world.*

Great moon goddess, I miss Mother terribly, and I really hope Kaira is wrong about her. That she had a good reason for having left us at the mercy of the Storm Wolves pack.

The air remains still tonight, and it feels like I'm suffocating on my breath. I'm staring out into the wilderness over the cliff. There's nothing but blackness. I just needed some time away from the guys, some breathing space, and time to gather myself.

Part of me suspects that if I don't get myself under control, that I will stand no chance of saving Kaira or keeping Jae safe. So I need to find a way to cope with everything.

But it isn't long before the soft crunch of foliage sounds behind me, and I twist around. Ragnar marches in my direction, though by his loud exhales, I'm guessing he freaked about me missing.

I want to apologize, to say I'm sorry, except I'm struggling with my thoughts right now.

"Little fox," he says, and all I can see beneath the silvery hue of the moonlight are those haunting blue eyes, his short brown hair framed around his face.

I expect a sleuth of I-told-you-so's and reminders that I shouldn't go off on my own.

"Don't," I tell him, stealing his chance. "I know what you're going to say."

"Is that so?" He takes a seat next to me and drops his arms over his bent legs. Instead of talking, he just sits in silence with me, looking out into the darkness of the land beyond the cliff.

I sense Ragnar staring at me, and I glance over, but never in a hundred years did I expect anyone to be looking at me with adoration. Let alone him. Not after what we went through. Not after everyone's plans failed because of me. And certainly not after I got us all cursed.

There is something deep and alluring in his expression, and part of me wishes that my fated mate had stared at me this way on our first night together. That he hadn't been so drunk that he only wanted to fuck my brains out or freaked out when he found out I was also a witch.

That's the thing about the brutal Alphas in this world. They either want to own and fuck you to breed with you, or they sell you off, discard you.

But no matter how handsome Ragnar is, how many muscles he has, how he watches me like he might devour me, I need to remember who I'm dealing with and what his pack consists of...

Violent Alphas.

"What do you think the world was like before the virus killed nearly everyone?" he asks, turning his gaze to the blackness of space over the cliff.

Quickly adding two and two together, I realize he's trying to get me talking and to calm down. And it works. "I'm going to say amazing. From what I've read in books, things were easier. People were happier. For one, they had endless food they got from places called grocery stores. And they attended parks and fairs with friends."

He's studying me carefully, a smile curling the corners of his lips. "You seem to know quite a bit."

"I love to read. But can you imagine a world where it's safe to just walk down the road and not be attacked by wolves or zombies? Crazy, huh?" I laugh to myself. "Yep, a fantasy world right there. But that shit is long gone. We are the remnants of what was left after the virus killed everyone else. I wish I knew more, like if wolves lived in harmony with the humans back then."

"Whatever happened in the past, we are in a shit place now where zombies are taking over the south, and they are gonna be up here soon in droves," he states nonchalantly. "More reason to set up a sector where people follow one Alpha, and we fight against them. I've seen it done in the Shadowlands Sector successfully."

I feel his touch on my arm, and his warmth swims over my skin, but his words still bother me. "Easy for you to say when you're an Alpha. I don't stand much of a chance of a happy future. I'm an Omega and considered the lowest of the low. And because I'm a hybrid witch, I'm nothing but a target for everyone." I get to my feet, his hand falling away from my arm.

"That doesn't mean we can't continue an alliance after I help you get your sister back."

I adore his confidence, and I'm holding him to his word, but I've also learned that the universe is more reliable in letting me down.

"What do you want in exchange?" I ask warily.

"I'll be ruling the Savage territory, and you need a safe haven, right?"

I eye him carefully and get to my feet. "And in exchange you'll want my magic? Except, maybe that's not what I want."

A flash of hurt crosses his gaze as he climbs to his feet to join me, now towering over me. "So, what is it you want? Look around you, Narah. There is nowhere you and your sisters can hide. Omegas don't last long on their own. And once word spreads of your magic, you'll be hunted down and killed."

I hug myself and turn away from him, his words sharper than he knows. I've lived with that dread my entire life. "I want to be away from all the chaos and war. I'm tired of being hated for what I am. It's why I've kept my magic a secret for so long."

Half-witches, half-wolves like me and Kaira are worthless. It's why my fated mate rejected me, why I'm now fighting desperately to save my sisters. I've heard of a female sanctuary in Poland, but rumors can just as easily lead us astray and into danger.

Just as easily as Ragnar's offer of sanctuary. He hasn't even taken over the Savage Sector, and the Alphas who call this place home are murderers and would die before bowing the knee to another...let alone a foreigner like him. So, what would they do to me when he makes me use my magic?

It's a disaster waiting to happen. I'll be exposed, hated, and all I want is to slip under the radar with my sisters to survive. I've learned long ago that holding onto any kind of hope that my future will be anything but normal is me being foolish.

His shadow falls over me, and he puts his hands on my shoulders turning me to face him.

My heart beats loudly in my ears as I stare up at him. I hate myself for being so attracted to him at a time like this. Hate how my body leans toward him as if we're drawn to each other.

His hand moves to my neck, holding me in place. "You are mine. You gave me parts of yourself that were truly untouched. That's a gift that I will repay with protection." He traces the pads of his fingers gingerly over the curve of my neck where he'd bitten me. "My mark does more than mask your wolf's desperation for your fated mate. It makes every inch of you mine, and I have no intention of letting you go."

I should shove him away, but instead, I'm losing myself to him. Wanting the things his gaze promises. Everything about him is Alpha, masculine, dominating. There's a part of me that wants his protection for me and my sisters, but I'm also terrified it might be signing a death warrant.

"B-but that wasn't what we agreed. You said..." My breath catches in my throat at what he's saying.

"I said I'd help you, and that's what I did."

I'm shaking and fighting the way my wolf surges through me to get closer to his... and of course, I should have understood. She no longer craves my soulmate, Martell, but now pines for Ragnar. The call is not as painful as it had been for my fated mate, but I see now how submissive I am to my primal instincts.

"I gave you what you wanted, but there was only one way to do that." The sharp, serious expression he sports intensifies as his hold tightens like he's scared I'm going to run from him.

"W-why? Why would you do that? You don't even know me," I whisper, trying to pull away from him while he holds me close.

"Every wolf has a thirst to find someone to call their own, and everything about you makes me want to dominate you. Adore you. Fuck you."

I shudder with that feeling where my body tingles. He brushes the loose strands of hair out of my face. "Thing is that when an Omega gives herself to an Alpha, it doesn't make them powerless. It's a gift they've given the Alpha to be protected and cherished."

My face flushes at words I don't expect or deserve. His hands fall to my waist, and he's close to me. Everything in my mind screams to back away, but my body says *yes*.

I manage to shake my head. "No." I gasp the word as if it's the hardest thing I've ever had to do.

His eyes are wild. "I won't let anyone hurt you ever again." He leans closer to me, his voice deepening. "I won't abandon you, but you need to trust me."

I can't move. Not even if I tried...

His chest heaves against mine, his grip tightening. Fire burns in his gaze, and it awakes my arousal. He knows what he wants, and he takes it. I should loathe him for making me crave him, but how can I when he's eased the ache I carried for Martell?

Instead of breaking away, I relax a little bit and let out a breath.

We're not fated mates. That connection isn't there, but the pull I feel toward him is undeniable.

Suddenly, he's kissing me, claiming me. His teeth tug at my bottom lip, his fingers twirling in my hair and clenching into a fist, holding me as he licks into my mouth. There are no words for the way he kisses me, the dominant way he's taking what he wants... me.

It's impossible to resist him.

His hands move to the sides of my face, and I'm lost in his kiss. He walks me back until I am nestled against a tree. My heart skips a beat, and I tug on his shirt, fisting the fabric, drawing him closer. The way he kisses me is powerful and overwhelming. For so long, I never knew what I'd been missing by not being with a man like him. How much I've been starved of affection.

I don't even know how long we've been kissing... a minute, an hour, but I'm completely lost, and even if I remembered why I had to pull away from him now, it's too late. The heady smell of desire overwhelms me.

I kiss him back, needing more. Even if my mind demands I back off, I don't think I can. Moans roll out of my throat as his mouth moves to my neck, taking small nips. His hands fall to my waist, and he tugs open the buttons on my pants. Crouching in front of me, he pushes them down my legs in seconds; I step out of them as I kick off my shoes. He moves so fast, sliding my underwear down my legs and off. His gaze pauses on the spot between my legs and licks his lips.

His tongue is on my pussy without warning. A wicked tongue that knows what he's doing.

"Ahh," I moan, my legs quivering as he sucks on me. There's no relenting, this man understands my needs, and he is enjoying himself. He holds onto my hips again, his fingers digging into my skin.

I open my mouth to say something, but only moans spill out. He picks up speed, his tongue flicking over my clit, pushing me right to the edge where I'm beyond control.

I'm there, falling, tumbling into the abyss of a building orgasm. I fist his hair, my cries growing louder when he finally releases me and stands with a growl from his throat.

With rough hands, he tugs me away from the tree.

"I don't want you cut up by the bark when I fuck you."

I desperately fist his shirt and haul him over to me, our mouths clashing. "Make me forget everything," I whisper against his mouth.

"Good girl."

I close my eyes, tilting my head back, and give myself to him. His tongue traces the curve of my throat, his hands on my breasts, squeezing. His words float on the air, "You are mine."

The sounds of his belt unbuckling and his zipper coming down have me eager for him. "Every girl needs a good fucking." His large hands are on the back of my thighs, and I'm lifted off my feet.

Quickly, I wrap my arms around his neck as he steps away from the tree. I coil my legs around his hips, his cock already teasing the heat of my pussy.

A moan spills from my mouth, and he growls. "Fuck, I love the sounds you make."

His mouth finds me, and he kisses me like I belong to him, rough and demanding. He doesn't ask but takes what he wants. For him, it all comes down to control. He's powerful and terrifying, but with me, he treats me like I'm glass.

He pushes into me quickly, the sensation of his cock sliding inside of me, leaves me breathless. He is a very large man and forces himself to fit inside me.

I cry out. He's not taking it slow, and I love it. He cups my ass, takes a deep breath, then drives me against him.

His strength is crazy as he holds me in his arms while standing and fucks me with extraordinary power, his hips rocking into me over and over. The pain he causes, the pleasure he delivers, is indescribable. He picks up speed, his growls filling my ears.

I'm wrapped around him, our bodies plastered together, and I look deep into his blue eyes.

His jaw clenches every time he thrusts into me, and I moan, taking him completely.

"There's something about you, little fox. Something I can never give up." He groans and buries his face in my neck, where I feel his teeth grazing my skin. His sweet words engulf me. No one has ever spoken to me like this.

With those words comes an explosion that erupts within me and drives me over the edge I've been precariously balancing on. And when the burning pressure of his cock swells inside me and pushes against my inner walls, that's when my orgasm tears through me.

My cries are swallowed by his kiss as desire pulses through me, and Ragnar has his own roaring climax. He growls, and I feel his seed filling me, pulsing, and there's so much.

He's tense and holding me tightly, coming for a long time. We're locked in place, both of us united.

His growl vibrates against me.

I close my eyes and tuck my face into the curve of his neck. He's buried deep within me and his bulging knot is tightly fit inside me, keeping us bound. I never understood how knotting really worked, just that it was another way for Alphas to lay claim on Omegas and give their seed a better chance of getting the female pregnant. Lucky for me, I made sure to take a special herb for a month leading up to my ceremonial night with Martell... a herb that aids in me not falling pregnant for a couple of months afterward.

I wasn't a fool to fall pregnant so quickly in a new relationship.

Ragnar has his lips at my ear, distracting me, and he asks, "Are you okay, little fox?"

"Yes," I respond, then he kisses me again, leaving me breathless. We'll be together for half an hour, maybe longer, connected this way until my muscles relax, until his knotted cock unswells, and as crazy as it sounds, I love this bonding time with him.

"I want you to rest now, to let go. I've got you."

We are looking at each other, and there's something ridiculously intimate about having an Alpha's cock locked inside you. Where it feels like I've got the upper hand and he's at my mercy...that's what I tell myself as I lean against him, my arms draping over his shoulders. I wonder why the universe didn't send someone like him to me as my fated mate?

It's only then, when I glance up, that I meet Crius' gaze.

My breath catches in my throat. How long has he been watching us?

He's standing amid the shadows, watching us with a dark expression. And... is that his hand down his pants?

5

CRIUS

othing's worse than waking up with your mouth tasting like you've just been licking dirt.

I chew on my fifth jerky strip, unable to get rid of the funky taste. What I wouldn't give for a bucket of hot coffee. Black, no sugar. And I'm salivating. Another reason to get our asses back into town and out of these fucking woods.

I've had six hours to sleep off the shit-fest from yesterday. Don't get me wrong, I'm still pissed how things turned out with the witches, but like Ragnar had told me, it wasn't the time for me to use my magic. Especially not when it would have meant that Narah's sister might have ended up as collateral damage.

Really, I shouldn't care. I came on this mission with the promise of carrying out a spell that would aid Ragnar in winning over the witches. Of course, it came at my expense, yet Ragnar kept telling me to wait after Narah's sister made her presence known.

But we're going back to the witches, and next time, I won't be holding back. I don't give an iota what anyone thinks, won't let anyone stand in my way.

Chewing on the food, I lift my gaze to Narah stumbling out of the woods and coming toward the campsite. Her hair's mussed and eyes wild. Goddess, she's gorgeous. She's wearing the same clothes as yesterday, tight pants over long legs, shirt, and leather vest taut over the curve of her breasts. Like the rest of us, I'm dying for a hot bath upon our return to town. Preferably with her by my side.

Is it crazy that she's the first thing to have brought excitement to my day?

And now I can't get the image of her from last night being fucked by Ragnar out of my mind. Those sounds she made, the beautiful look on her face as she rode his cock and finally came. One could easily lose their heads to a girl like her, which I suspect Ragnar might be doing.

But it's not my business. These idiots in the pack have their own darkness to deal with. Ragnar and his asshole father. Nikos, the outcast who's forced to live with his family's enemy. And Stone who has always struggled with finding his place in the world and is constantly angry about it. It's like he just doesn't fit in, but I think he's searching for something he hasn't found... a reason to belong.

Don't I fucking know that feeling.

I've accepted my fate and the broken past that I can't undo. Which is why I decided to carry out the spell to help my friends. I've come to peace with that decision... even if it might end in my demise. It's a risk I agreed to take, regardless of the outcome.

I exhale loudly. The dark thoughts creeping forward. My brother's blood on my hands. His death haunts me. I close my eyes, fighting the gaping hole splitting open in my soul. It's ripped me apart, and there is no way of putting me back together again. Not after what I did.

Most days, the smile I wear is all that holds me together.

"Hey, where is everyone?" Narah asks from across the clearing. Her sweet voice slices through my thoughts, and I welcome the distraction. I welcome her. Anything to stop myself from drowning.

I open my eyes and glance over at her. "Meditating."

"Sure." She doesn't believe me, and that's fine. I wouldn't either. But I smile, plastering on the face I wear for everyone because no one wants a fucking sorrowful bastard hanging around with them.

"Come and eat something," I say. "The other three guys are finishing packing up camp and have gone to fill up our water skins."

"Well, that explains why I couldn't find Ragnar."

Exhaling loudly, I stuff more of the jerky into my mouth and reach into the bag for the bread, hoping that might help with the taste in my mouth. My eyes never leave her though, not the way she strolls over, her hips swaying, her hands by her sides while she scans the woodland. There's something so alluring about this girl, even when she looks startled.

Who am I kidding? I love seeing her scared. That is why my wolf went for her yesterday.

I offer her an open bag of jerky. "Help yourself. It'll grow hair on your chest." I smack my lips, to which she rolls her eyes.

"Coffee would be heaven right now." She takes a piece and bites down on it, then pulls at it.

I laugh. "The jerky's a tough sonofabitch."

She wrestles with it but doesn't give up and finishes it. "About last night," she starts, her cheeks blushing.

"You had an amazing time," I answer while grinning. "Did Ragnar not tell you we share everything, and that includes watching?"

Looking mortified, eyes wide, she shrugs. "Sort of worked it out, but it's unusual."

She reaches for another piece of dried meat and glances around the woods, then looks back at me. "Hope you don't mind me asking, but what happened yesterday with the witches and you... you know, afterward?" Her forehead creases, and she's wearing an apologetic look on her face. "Sorry, maybe I shouldn't ask. Nikos told me not to ask you."

Urgh. Of course, he would. I stuff the rest of the food into the bag and zip it up.

"Sometimes I lose control."

"Next time, maybe don't hit the crazy button around me if your wolf sees me as a meal," she teases, smiling. Though, I can tell it's an awkward smile.

"I'm pretty sure if I caught you, I would have either licked you or tried to hump you."

Her mouth drops open, looking partially horrified. "Are you joking?"

I chuckle. "If only I was. My wolf is a horny bastard. Doesn't help that you always smell so delicious." I find myself gravitating to her. She doesn't back away, and I'm impressed by her resolve. "You don't need to fear me. Trust me, there are many things I want to do to you, but killing you isn't one of them."

Her cheeks blush. I adore her innocence. That deep inside, she's wholesome. And while she might disagree, she is not broken in my eyes, but absolutely perfect, just like those kissable lips.

I've kissed my fair share of women in my life, but something tells me once I taste her, I'd do anything to claim her.

And I already have enough crap clouding my head to drag her into the shithole that I've fallen into. So I turn from her, not wanting to complicate things or let her believe I can promise anything beyond the here and now.

She snatches my wrist and says, "You never answered my question. What happened back at the coven? What were you trying to do?"

I don't move but focus on the point of contact where her small hand wraps around my arm, and how such a small hand radiates intense heat. Her fingers twitch like she's trembling. It is ridiculous that such a touch should affect me in any way but draw my attention. Except I'm breathing in her scent while my heartbeat thumps harder.

I turn to her, and she's still holding onto me. Her eyes are swimming in curiosity, and I swallow the thickness in my throat at how easily she makes me forget what she asked me.

"Always keep your tender heart protected, gorgeous girl. In this life, everyone will try to tear it apart for their own gain."

She blinks, confused, and I don't blame her. I have no idea where that bit of philosophical crap just came from. She brings things out of me I never expect, like this overbearing instinct to keep her protected. To ensure the vulnerable girl remains that way for as long as possible.

"I'll take it into consideration," she answers and releases my hand.

I laugh at her tenacity and stubbornness.

"But it's not what I asked."

"And just like your persistence, I am now going to return to packing up because the guys are back." Their scent wafts on the light breeze.

She lifts her gaze just as they emerge from the dense woods, carrying filled water skins.

When she glances back at me, there's a disappointed expression painting her face. I shouldn't care. No. I don't give a shit if she's happy about me dismissing her question. Not at fucking all. Opening up won't serve any purpose but make me care for her more, have her stare at me with pity in her eyes.

I've left a trail of broken hearts behind me because if there's one thing I know, it's that I don't do long-term. I have no plans for a future, and I'm not dragging anyone into my mess. I doubt Narah here is a girl who does anything but long-term commitment.

Against my better judgment and telling myself not to get involved with her more than I have to, I say, "Don't look so sad, gorgeous, or you'll shatter me." I grin at her and move to toss more dirt over the fire's ashes with my foot.

"I know you're scared to open up, but it's not that hard. I mean, I'll start. I'm terrified of bumping into my ex again, scared out of my mind that my wolf will grow so submissive in his presence that I'll hand myself over to him. Then he'll try to kill me again," she says behind me, her voice soft and carries a slight tremble.

Her words touch me, fueling my anger that her soul-mate made this beautiful girl so petrified. If I ever find him... he won't even see me coming before I rip him to shreds. What she doesn't know is that she has nothing to worry about from him if we're around.

When I glance over my shoulder at her, she's actually pouting at me. "Narah, babe, I'm doing you a favor by not opening up."

"Is that so?" She arches a thin eyebrow.

I really don't get why she's so persistent. "Yep. If I do, you'll fall head over heels for my charm, and I would hate to leave you broken-hearted."

She bursts out laughing, and I fucking adore her. I'm laughing with her when the others approach.

"What's so funny?" Stone asks.

"Crius told a joke," Narah says, accepting the water skin Ragnar hands her, then drinks several mouthfuls of water.

"Really?" Stone's voice climbs. "Hope it wasn't one of your dumb fart jokes." He chuckles to himself.

Ass.

I get to work, and it isn't long before we're all hiking through the woods once more. A full day passes without a single incident.

"The witches really want your sister, Narah," Nikos states. "Seeing as they've kept us alive this entire trip out of the woods."

He and Narah continue chatting, while I take the lead with Ragnar as we emerge from the forest. The late afternoon sun burns brightly just over the horizon of treetops, the sky streaked in pinks and oranges, while to our right, the sky darkens with the promise of a storm.

"Perfect timing to reach town," I mutter and glance over to Ragnar deep in his own thoughts, his brow pinched. "Where's your head at? Still buried between Narah's legs?" I tease.

He cuts me a sharp look. "Did you enjoy yourself, watching?"

He almost sounds jealous, which isn't like him. "Fuck yeah, I did. You almost sound pissed. Has she made you soft? Get your head on straight."

"My head is exactly where it needs to be."

"Could've fooled me. Looks a little lopsided," I counter, realizing how lame I sound with that comeback. "Anyway, what's our plan tonight? Food, sleep, then—"

"Then we leave at dawn for Black Hallows."

I smirk. "Shit, man, you're going to see *her*."

"Shut the hell up. We're going to ask her for a favor to track down Narah's mother."

Thankfully, I'm not the one who's fallen head over heels for a hybrid like Narah, then intend to take her into a village where Ragnar had to practically promise marriage to the seer living there for information from her when we first arrived in Romania. He hasn't returned since, so this should be a fun trip.

The closer we get to town, the stronger the smells of roasting meat and fire fill the air. My stomach rumbles. Stone is by our side now as we walk along the dirt track, peppered with establishments tailored for Alphas.

Whorehouses, bars, inns, and places to buy almost anything you need. I never thought I'd be so happy to see such a rundown shithole like this. Anything is better than being in those fucking cursed woods, that's for sure.

"I'm so hungry," Stone groans. "Tonight, I'm going to eat one of those suckling pigs all on my own."

"By the size of you, I won't be surprised. And you're getting a gut, man." I poke fun at him.

"Fuck off. I've seen you finish off an entire turkey on your own, so don't even start," Stone snaps.

I glance back at Nikos and Narah strolling behind us. Her eyes skate to mine, making me instantly scorching hot. Of course, I should keep my distance, but I also can't resist playing with her because I'm tortured that way. And really, she's the only thing that seems to distract my mind from everything else, and I like that.

When I blow her a kiss, she shows me the finger, and I suck in a deep breath, turning away, grinning.

We walk right past the inn where we'd stayed the night of our trip and keep trekking to the end of the road to a wooden cottage where Jae is being protected.

We step up onto the porch, only to find the front door ajar. There are no guards out front either, and an uneasy feeling curls down my spine.

I reach over to grab Ragnar by the shoulder to stop him, but he's already barging into the wooden cabin.

He pauses in the entryway, and I don't even need to see it. The metallic tang of blood hits me hard.

My stomach drops, and when Narah starts screaming behind me, my heart splinters into a thousand pieces.

Ragnar steps into the cabin and the massacre that greets us sickens me.

Blood.

Dead bodies.

The furniture turned over, the walls scratched, everything demolished.

"Jae!" Narah is bellowing, and I look over my shoulder at her in Nikos' arms, struggling for release. He's taking her away from the carnage. My chest is hurting from her agony.

"What the fuck happened here!" Ragnar roars, and I rush inside, scanning the place for Jae, praying I don't find her.

6

NARAH

"Put me down," I cry, shoving against Nikos, while he has his arm looped around my middle and is lifting me off the ground. He carries me away from the cabin that smells of death and blood, and I scream at him.

It's where we left my sister to be protected, but this is the farthest from keeping her safe, isn't it?

I can't even see straight, not when my insides feel like my heart's burst and I'm bleeding to death.

"Narah, please, just let the guys check it's safe first," Nikos keeps telling me, but I'm so angry, I keep bucking against him to let me go.

I punch, scratch, and pull at the arm he has locking me in place as tears roll down my face. "Jae," is what I keep saying and, "Let me go."

Power surges across my fingertips.

White lines dance over my hands, and Nikos flinches.

"I wouldn't do that if you were you," he threatens, not releasing his hold.

"Then release me," I hiss.

"Narah," Ragnar's voice streams from the cabin, and I shoot him a glance as he marches across the yard toward us. His shoulders are curved forward, his face looking defeated, and I burst into more tears.

Goddess, please not Jae.

My feet touch the ground, but I'm using Nikos to lean against and to stand upright. It's as if I no longer have any bones in my body, and everything inside me aches.

"Your sister isn't in the cabin," Ragnar says firmly.

I freeze, pushing away from Nikos, and stumble to Ragnar. "W-what... where is she?" I'm running before they can stop me.

Ragnar is saying something behind me, but I don't hear him. I race right past Crius and burst into the cabin where Stone's crouching by a man who's gurgling blood.

It takes me a moment to comprehend what I'm looking at. My senses are on overload, while the pungent scent of blood strangles me. More tears prick my eyes. I hate feeling so lost, so petrified.

I swallow hard, fighting the panic as I search the room. Two enormous men are strewn on the floor, their limbs twisted. One has a lethal gash across his throat, his skin torn and ripped as if ravaged by wolves, while a blade sticks out of the chest of the second guy.

The harsh afternoon light coming through the dirty windows makes everything look sickly yellow. I rush through the room, pushing aside turned furniture. "Jae!" When I don't find her in the main room, I dart into the bedroom and bathroom.

Empty.

I spin on the spot in the small hallway and the cabin tilts around me. Of course, Ragnar told me Jae wasn't here, but I had to check for myself. Growing up, Jae had been an expert at hide-n-seek, and I always had to triple-check to find her in the most unusual places. Still, my chest aches so much I can barely draw in breath.

I clench my fists and hold them to my stomach as I fall to my knees and the tears keep flowing. Who took my sister? Fucking men... it's always them, taking any Omega they find for rutting, for breeding.

Darkness swallows me, and I lean forward, crying hard, my entire body shaking while dread races through my veins. The guilt that I left her behind burns through me, stealing my breath, stealing my logic.

She couldn't have gone into the woods with us, but... I can't cope with losing her again.

A hand rubs my back. "Narah," Stone says softly, and he wraps me in his arms.

I fall into them and let him hold me as I cry against his chest, as images of Jae being terrified flood my head.

Stone holds me, stroking my back, and doesn't say a word. I don't know how long I've been crying for when I finally open my sore eyes and stare up at him.

"D-did he say anything about who took Jae?" I glance into the main room to where the gurgling guy now lies dead.

"They were ambushed by six men, but he had no clue who they were. No packs were mentioned, no names, nothing. They attacked earlier today, killed everyone, and took your sister." His voice is grave, and I hiccup another cry that spills past my lips.

"Someone must have seen something. It's broad daylight," I murmur, and I clutch onto this shirt desperately.

"That's what we're going to find out. I promise you, we'll find those assholes and destroy them," he growls. He lifts me to my feet and guides me outside, where I stumble out of his arms, drawing in fresh air.

The first drop of rain lands on my nose. I look up at the tainted clouds smearing the sky, turning the afternoon an ashen color, matching the darkness consuming me.

I bring my attention to the four Alphas standing in the yard, looking as miserable as I feel. Those dead men are their pack members, and their loss must be killing them.

Wildfire burns behind Ragnar's gaze, fury darkening his face. "Stone, take her to the inn," he commands while holding my stare. I'm falling apart, and I can't even find it in me to speak. Then he turns to Crius and Nikos. "You two are with me."

I don't remember moving, but the next thing I know, Stone and I are walking into a room at the inn. It's stale in here, dust covers the tops of the dresser and book-shelf. I keep looking at the bed, remembering the night before we left to find the witches, where Jae and I had stayed up chatting about her trip into the Shadowlands Sector. About how much I missed her. About how we'd never be apart again. I made a promise and broke it almost as fast as I'd made it.

"We should be out there," I say, turning to Stone, who shuts the door behind us. "I need to search for Jae. Maybe she's being held captive in this inn?" My mind is racing, and I'm buzzing with desperation and adrenaline. I want to run from room to room and check for her. I need to find her. Instead, I start pacing back and forth across the room. I even pop into the bathroom and grab a towel to dry the rain from my hair and off my face.

Stone somehow keeps himself calm as he strolls toward me.

Without saying a word, he takes my hand and leads me to the table and chairs near the large window that overlooks the main street below. "From up here, we have a vantage point if anything goes down. Ragnar is a ruthless hunter, and if he tracked down Jae the first time in south Romania with no real clues, trust me, he'll find her again."

I blink, waiting for my tears to stop falling, then turn my attention to the window. Down below, there's a single man sauntering toward the tavern across from the inn. Otherwise, there's no one around.

"Maybe they're long gone," I say. "We should go after them."

"Where to?" he asks, standing right next to me. "Running around frantically isn't the answer. It might feel like the right thing to do, but trust me, it's not. Once we find information, we'll track her. Someone would have noticed six men entering town, and we'll discover who, even if it means burning down this entire town."

I nod, but my stomach remains in knots. It's bad enough that we're cursed, but now we've lost Jae. I never seem to catch a break.

The rain has picked up and hits the window outside. A storm is coming, and I watch the droplets sliding down the glass remembering how Kaira and Jae loved watching drops racing down the windows when it rained. How they'd try to each pick the first droplet to reach the bottom of the window.

My throat tightens, and more tears spill down my cheeks as fast as the rain.

Lightning forks across the sky. Seconds later, the boom of thunder rattles the walls surrounding us.

I fall into my seat, my hands trembling as I hold them in my lap. "I hate to admit it, but I know you're right. I just feel like I'm dying on the inside from doing nothing."

Stone pulls up a seat next to me and we both stare outside where the rain pours down, fat drops plinking against the window.

I turn to him. "I'm sorry about the loss of your pack members."

"I'm going to slaughter whoever did this. They were decent men." He quiets after that and looks out at the raging storm blowing through town.

I try to make sense of everything that's happened. Kaira. That Mother is still alive. Jae being kidnapped. Sometimes things are just too overwhelming, but then I remember the vision I had not too long ago while I was doing a tarot reading for a client. And my words escape past my lips.

"I think I foresaw some of this danger coming my way," I mutter.

"How?" Stone asks.

"In a vision." I clench my fists in my lap, thinking back to the vision. "I was in the woods, and Kaira was there, wearing strange markings on her face. She was really evil and kept laughing as a great wolf attacked Jae, and... it ripped her throat out." My heart hammers in my ears.

"Do you often have visions?" He shuffles his chair closer to me and curls an arm around my shoulders. I let him draw me into his embrace. I welcome the comfort, the warmth, anything to avoid feeling like I'm being hollowed out from the inside.

I shake my head no. "First time. But it's been on my mind since I saw Kaira with the witches and how different she behaved. And now Jae's gone. Goddess, you don't think the witches did this? Spelled some random guys to go get my sister?" I suddenly feel sick, and I wrap an arm around my middle.

Stone strokes my hair, and he wraps me up. "I doubt it. If they had, they would have eliminated us in the woods already."

I'm nodding, but I'm not sure what to believe anymore. I just close my eyes and let Stone's touches calm my breathing. He doesn't give me words of reassurance, but he stays by my side. His presence alone is everything to me. I grew up not putting faith in anyone but my sisters, and now with these Viking Alphas... They've shown me a part of themselves I never expected. A caring, tender side that has me clinging to them. Who would have thought Stone would be such a teddy bear, especially after I've seen him in battle? He's a savage.

The next hour moves excruciatingly slow. Stone and I barely exchange any words, and mostly that's on me. I'm too busy panicking and staring out the window.

When I spot Ragnar, Crius, and Nikos emerge from the tavern and cross the road toward the inn, I shoot to my feet. "They're coming back."

Stone is already bursting out of the room, I guess to greet them as they wouldn't know what room we're in.

Moments later, all four enter the room.

I leap to my feet, rushing over to them, staring from one face to the next. "What did you find?" The words are out of my mouth before they even shut the door.

Ragnar answers, "A couple at the tavern saw the strangers enter town and go straight to the cabin like they knew exactly where they were going." His lips pinch as irritation paints over his expression. "They said a local man at the tavern apparently spoke with them as they left town, and they had a girl with them."

I gasp, stepping closer, my pulse beating so fast the room is spinning. "And?" I'm holding my breath, unable to inhale until I hear his words.

"No one knows where the man lives, but he's a regular and comes in most days. He's never missed a night for a few drinks. So, we wait for him to return."

His words keep playing over in my head, as desperation blooms in my mind. "That's too much time to wait. One of us should wait for him and the rest of us go into the woods after them. We've all got her scent. Can we follow that?"

"Not with this rain, we can't," Nikos informs me.

I'm shaking, and my fingers play with the hem of my vest, tugging at the loose strands, while I'm fighting to not cry. Heat spreads through my chest, and I stumble back to the window, feeling completely lost. Completely empty. Completely heartbroken.

What choice do I have? I keep repeating in my mind.

I know what Ragnar will say. That we'll run around in the woods blindly, except sitting here waiting, is going to kill me.

My heart beats so fast, the sound of my racing pulse whirring in my ears.

"Narah, I promise we will find her," Ragnar says.

But when I turn to face him, I must have moved too fast because the room suddenly tilts around me, and darkness gathers at the edge of my vision, stealing everything.

The last thing I see is Ragnar lunging for me as my world blacks out.

7

NARAH

The fiery blaze licks the cold from my body.

It crackles and spits embers into the night sky, the soft rain doing nothing to put out the flames.

After passing out from the panicked shock of my sister being kidnapped, I woke up and realized that I won't be of any help to anyone if I make myself sick with worry.

So now, I'm standing several feet away from the shore of the river where Ragnar, Nikos, Stone, and Crius push a small boat out into the water. The dead bodies of their pack members lay inside, wrapped in fabric. And as is tradition, they light the boat on fire.

The night comes alive with the inferno, and it draws the locals from town who've crowded around to watch the Viking cremation ceremony for the dead. These strangers whisper in the background to each other as if this were entertainment for them. There are about a dozen of them, all male, and being the only female leaves me feeling highly uncomfortable.

Every time I glance back, I notice three men staring at me lecherously, rather than paying attention to the ceremony. They make my skin crawl.

Ragnar and his men break into a sorrowful song, and I turn back around to watch them. It starts off as a hum and climbs in volume, the tune slow and heartfelt. It touches me in ways I don't expect, my chest tightening, and I swallow past my thickening throat. I don't understand the words, but in my mind, I imagine it's a farewell song to the dead. With it, my gut churns with guilt because these men lost their lives while protecting my sister... for me.

So many lives are lost in this world. My thoughts circle back to Jae and Kaira, and how I never want to say farewell to them in such a way. It would destroy me.

The night seems to be closing in around me; the smoke choking me, the storm growling overhead, and that overwhelming panic surges through me once more.

Deep breaths. I take them in slowly, needing to calm down.

Yet, each time I look at the burning boat, my heart beats furiously. It's a simple fishing boat made of wood and all Ragnar could find at the last minute. Stone had told me they normally layer the dead with jewels before the cremation, but with them having none here, I helped them collect wildflowers to use as a replacement.

I tilt my head up at the black plume of smoke... *it will carry the deceased to the afterlife,* Stone had told me.

The song pauses, and Ragnar steps closer to the water's shore. He begins to speak in a language I don't understand. Maybe Danish or Ancient Norse. But whatever he's saying, my eyes prick at the agony in his voice. The pain of loss.

As hard as I try not to, my mind pictures Jae in the boat. I wouldn't have the strength to give such a speech if I lost her. I'm shaking just thinking about it.

Ragnar falls silent, and he bends down to grab a handful of dirt, then straightens. He tosses it into the water. Each of his men does the same, and then Nikos returns to my side, his eyes glinting against the burning pyre.

"Why did you throw soil into the water?" I point my chin to the river.

He leans in closer, our shoulders touching, and whispers, "In Denmark, it's a symbol to the gods for their blessing to keep those alive with us longer. Would you like to do it and show your respect?"

I nod. "Would that be okay?"

"Of course."

I walk steadfastly to the water's edge and crouch down, scooping up a handful of the muddy earth. It's cold and almost liquid in my hand. Then I toss the soil into the river, where it lands with a loud splash.

I murmur under my breath, "May the deceased find peace in the afterlife. And please... don't ever take my sisters from me." The words stick to the back of my throat and tears collect in my eyes. The hurt and pain of everything we've gone through bubbles to the surface, the memories of them taken from me are like barbed wire tearing across my mind.

I retreat from the river, lowering my head and blinking away the tears.

Nikos stands several feet away waiting for me, and a wry smile crosses his face as I join him. The other three are already strolling toward town, lost in their own grief.

"I didn't even know the men who lost their lives," I say. "Yet I can't stop crying or thinking, what if that was my sister out there on the boat?"

Nikos stares at me for a long while before responding, his shoulders slumped. I'm not used to seeing him this way. He's normally more confident and sure of himself.

"My mother would tell me that death will leave a broken heart, but love will always leave a memory no one can take from you."

"That's so beautiful and sad." I tuck those words away in my mind, needing to remind myself of them on the days when I think I can't go on. And it makes me wonder how much heartache Nikos lives with to hold onto such words too.

He lifts his eyes and gazes out at the river, shadows gliding across his hardened face. "She lost her family to war, then was forced to marry my father for survival. He treated her as well as any brutal Alpha does, but she told me she found her joy when I was born. She still found a way to look at the beauty and positivity in the world amid so much death and chaos. She never forgot her family, even if she watched them get butchered in pack combat. I often think of her when I feel myself falling apart."

I move my hand to his, taking it in mine. We stand in silence and stare out at the burning boat as it floats down the river and out of sight.

"I'm sorry," I finally say, unsure of what you're supposed to say in such a situation.

"Nothing to be sorry about. Fucked up shit happens to every single one of us, and those of us who survive have to find a way to live with it."

"And this is why the world is as broken as it is. All of us have major issues in our heads." I half-laugh at how pathetic that sounds.

"You're definitely right there." His grin warms me, and I'd rather see him smiling than be sorrowful. "Tonight we're going to wait in the tavern for the guy who spoke to your sister's kidnappers, and then we'll find her." His tone grows thick, as if he's fighting his own grief.

"How close were you and those three men?"

"Close enough to have met their parents and siblings."

I nod and lean against him, letting him know I'm here for him. Sometimes that's the best you can do when everything else is falling apart around you. Father once told me that grief is all the love I want to give but can't.

It's the built-up agony of not being able to share how much someone means to me.

Rain comes down harder now, as though the universe waited for the ceremony to end. The few locals who stayed to watch the fire are rushing back to town. We stand at the water's edge for a few more moments in silence.

"Let's head back." Nikos' hand curls tighter around mine and he guides us back through the dark woods.

The tension never leaves my body: for the lost lives, for my sister kidnapped, for what's yet to come.

I just need my sisters by my side, and then I'll be the happiest person in the world.

Once we reach the clearing that backs onto the rear of the tavern, I spot Ragnar, who looks back at us from amid the crowd of men that were at the funeral. He signals to Nikos with a flick of his hand, then points to the tavern. The three of them stroll inside. I look down at my free hand, still covered in mud and feeling sticky. I glance around for water and spot a tap just to the side of the tavern.

"Hey, give me a sec," I say and dart over to scrub the mess off my hands, figuring we're probably going to eat.

Nikos joins me, both of us scrubbing the dirt away under the running water, our hands touching, gently pushing each other aside. It's the first time since we arrived back in town that I've remembered I should be wearing my gloves. The top half of my fingers are stained black from magic, but luckily it's too dark for anyone else to see them. Though I'm surprised Nikos isn't freaking out about them at all.

In the woods, he was standoffish, but now he's different. There's a vulnerability to him, his walls lowered for a change. I guess attending a funeral makes people soften.

Without warning, he splashes me in the face.

I flinch and laugh. "Hey, that's how wars start. And you may not know this, but I am the queen of water bombs."

He chuckles. "Bring it on."

The splash of footsteps behind Nikos has me lifting my gaze over his shoulder, half expecting one of the other men coming to find out why we're dragging our feet.

But suddenly there is a rush of movement, a swish of air coming right at us, moving so fast, and I respond too slow.

Three strange men tackle Nikos, and an arm locks around his throat, his knees knocked out from under him. He hits the ground with a growl, and I stumble backward, shock strangling the breaths out of me. Two of them start hammering punches into Nikos' face and gut. He grunts and throws back hits, but he's overpowered fast.

I scream and rush toward them, power already racing down my arms. I don't care how haywire it goes, I'll burn down the whole freaking town if it means these three get the fuck away from us.

On my next step, one of the men swings around, his fist cracking me in the side of the head. It comes so hard and unexpected that I trip over my own feet, literally falling sideways and to the ground.

Burning pain spikes through my head, like my skull's been split in half and my brain is spilling out. I'm convinced that's what's happening as I cry out and reach for my head. But there's no blood.

The world spins around me, everything growing blurry. My head throbs like there's a heart inside it, thumping loudly.

Hands are yanking me off the ground. Pushing against my assailant, I recoil frantically but fall over again.

A shadow is cast over me as my vision comes back. A man stands above me and he shoves his foot down on my chest, pinning me to the ground.

"You're not going anywhere, Omega whore." The man spits the words at me, then sniffs the air. "I'm going to fuck you, then my friends will take their turn until there's nothing left of you."

I'm trembling, terror thundering through me. What the fuck!

That's when I get a better look at the man, at his broad chin, at his beady eyes, at his receding hairline. I recognize him instantly as one of the men watching me during the funeral ceremony. Bastards had been waiting for the right moment to attack.

It's what Alphas in the Savage Sector do. There's no top Alpha to command over them, so it's every man for himself. Each female is an object, whether she's with another man or not.

"Get the fuck off me," I wheeze, barely able to draw a breath from how heavily he presses down on me.

Lifting my hands, not even hesitating for a second, magical sparks leap from my fingertips. I shove my palms against his legs.

White zapping lines jolt up his legs, curling around them like serpents. He yelps and leaps off me, desperately patting his legs as if his pants are on fire.

My magic goes haywire and strands of power zap wildly from my hands, striking the back of the tavern, turning the whole stone wall black as if it's been burned to a crisp. Bits start falling away, creating tiny holes. Oh, shit.

I risk a fast glance over to Nikos, but all I see is a tangled ball of arms and legs, the growls from him deepen as they relentlessly beat into Nikos. But he gives just as good as he gets, and I can't tell who the heck is winning.

The other asshole is swinging back around and rushing at me madly. The hatred on his face terrifies me.

I scramble to my feet, but his fists collide with my chest.

The pain is explosive, and all the air rushes from my lungs in a tremendous gasp. I'm flying backward and smack into the ground hard. I cry out at the horrific pain sprawling across my chest, swallowing me. I can't suck in air, as though my lungs are frozen.

I lay on my back, my mouth opening and closing, and I smack a hand to my chest to breathe again.

The creep leans over me, laughing. He grabs at my hair with a fist and wrenches my head up off the ground. "Stop fighting, witch, or I'll cut your hands off." He shoves my head back down, and I wince at striking the hard surface again. He tears at my shirt, fabric ripping, the buttons under my vest popping.

Air slowly seeps into my lungs, and I wince while my hands push against him. But he shoves my arms away. He's pulling at the buttons on my pants, my whole body shuddering at how roughly he handles me.

Dread and fury collide within me.

I strike him with everything I have, shoving my hands into his face, kicking him. I lash out, scratching my nails down the side of his face, drawing blood, pulling his hair.

He growls and whacks my arm aside again. "Bitch, you'll be sorry you did that."

The look of death spreads over his face... my death.

He's going to murder me.

My heart thumps loudly in my ears as I crawl backward, dragging my ass away.

He lunges at me with the full force of a tornado, and I scream, jutting my hands in front of me, my skin tingling with magic.

Suddenly, the man flies backward and away from me, shock on his face, his wide eyes looking almost comical. He hits the ground devastatingly and groans in pain.

A huge, white wolf lunges out of the shadows and slams into the man so viciously that even from where I'm lying, I hear the crack of bones, the painful exhalation of air from crushed lungs.

I'm on my feet in moments, my pulse racing, but I can't move away. I freeze in place, staring at the wolf tearing into the man, claws and teeth shredding flesh, creating a gaping cavity in the middle of his chest.

My stomach rolls at the sight, and I look away quickly, only to discover the other two men lying in a heap of their own blood, their throats completely ripped out.

I shoot my attention back to Nikos in wolf form, destroying these men with such brutality that it should terrify me to my core. But I want him to hurt them, to tear them apart.

I've seen these Viking Alphas in their wolf forms battling the bears. These men specialize in battle. But this... I'm shocked at how easily Nikos rips their lives away without mercy. There is only anger and revenge, and it's beautiful.

He pauses, still standing atop the dead man and lifts his head up, then unleashes a haunting howl into the night.

Other howls in the distance sing back, connecting with him... there are so many out there that I have no idea how exactly my sisters and I will live safely without a pack's protection. I shake those thoughts away and study the massive wolf.

Rain pelts down on him, washing the blood from his mouth down his white fur.

Nikos is a wolf. A wild beast.

Every inch of him.

He's quiet most days, keeping to himself, but I see his true form now. The warrior who lays within, and how, despite everything, he's a survivor.

He turns his huge head in my direction and his eyes show the strength of this wolf, his soul, his heart. His ears are pointy, his teeth concealed, and he steps off the dead man, then makes his way toward me. His body contorts, fur vanishing, and in a few steps, he stands before me in his human form.

Naked.

Sexy as hell.

And so many muscles. He would easily put most men to shame with that ripped stomach, the strong chest, his biceps... goddess, everything about him is hard... including his cock. I gasp. Does that come after making a kill?

I quickly lift my eyes to look at where blood smears across his chest and mouth. Purple bruises under his eye and a bite mark scores his shoulder. A dark mark colors the side of his ribs, but somehow he's got no busted lip or nose.

"You're hurt." My words come out breathless. I'm not sure what makes me more shocked... his nakedness, his injuries, or how quickly he finished off three wolf shifters.

"I'll heal. Are you all right?"

I nod. "I'm fine."

"That fucking bastard, had no right ever touching you. I should have tortured him more, made him regret ever crossing us." His gaze sweeps over my body, pausing at the torn shirt under my vest. He reaches over and pulls at the fabric to straighten it, though with all the buttons gone, it's sort of useless. But the vest holds it in place. It will have to do.

"What you did is just... fearless."

He chuckles, then winces as his eye with the bruise squints. "I've never been called that before."

I slide a hand to the side of his face where he's injured. "Does it hurt?"

"I've had worse. And you know what they say... the more scars you have, the stronger your heart." He has his hands on my waist, and studies me like he might have missed an injury.

"I've never heard anyone say that before," I say.

"It's an old Norse proverb I've picked up, though I'm certain I'm butchering it. Words don't always stay in my head."

"Thank you for fighting for me."

His thumb strokes the skin he's found under my shirt over my hip bone. It sends tingles through me, the strange emotion of adrenaline and arousal tangling into a dangerous mix.

"They came so fast and scared the hell out of me," I murmur.

He's closer to me now, his breath on my face, and all I'm staring at are his lips, bits of blood at the corners of his mouth.

"The fault is mine for not keeping my guard up. This place is full of rogue Alphas and Betas who hunger for Omegas. But I won't let any of them touch you ever again."

His grip tightens, and I gasp. Something flares in his gaze, something primal. His wolf is there, still hyped up from the fight, and now Nikos stares at me like I'm his meal. His reward.

Both of us are bruised, him naked, me shaking, and we're standing in the dark. My heart is thundering in my chest at his touch, at how I can only focus on the point of contact where his fingers crawl across my stomach.

I don't push him away, not when I'm drowning in his attention. My nipples stiffen against the fabric of my shirt, and my mind is screaming to back the hell away as I find myself falling into his gaze. I shouldn't be turned on by any of these men, but each has a pull on me I don't want to understand.

"Back in the woods, you warned me about being with Ragnar and you three," I remind him, hoping it will force some logic into my lust-soaked brain too.

"I never said stay away from me." That cocky expression washes over his face.

Narrowing my gaze, I'm pretty sure he did mention me making a deal with all of them, but my head isn't exactly focused right now.

"I can smell your fear," he tells me, eyeing me from head to toe.

"I'm not afraid of you," I respond quickly, holding myself stiff. Thing is, I am shaking slightly because as strong as I act around these Alphas, they do scare me.

"That's not the kind of terror I'm talking about." He brings his face closer to mine, and for a ridiculous moment, I want to pretend this is real and that I have a man like Nikos in my life. Someone who fights to the death to protect me, whose stare alone has me imagining the dirtiest thoughts.

So much has happened in my life that in reality, I've never had much time to daydream about men. I accepted long ago my role is to be paired with someone I hoped would protect me and my sisters. But what I keep feeling around these four Vikings leaves me confused and constantly aroused.

"Then what kind of terror?" I breathe the words.

"You're scared to let yourself want me."

I roll my eyes extra hard to show him how far from the truth he is, except he laughs at me and my facade crumbles. So, I push myself forward and our mouths crush together. I can't help myself. His lips call to me, and he just saved my life.

His hungry fingers sweep around my back, pressing me tight against him, and he kisses me ravenously. He groans, licking my lips, and I taste the metallic blood of the other Alpha. The fact that I'm tasting it and kissing this hulking Viking excites me.

It's crazy the attraction I feel for this man I barely know. And the primal, guttural sounds he makes are so sexy. Goosebumps cover my skin with the heat building between us.

Flames ignite between my thighs, and I moan at the way his hand slides under my shirt and cups my breast.

"I love your body," he murmurs as he slides his hand down my stomach and pops open the button of my pants. His hand glides under the elastic of my underwear, holding my gaze. "It's perfect."

Something catches in my chest from his touch, from his words. I grew up never being told I was beautiful or anything along those lines. Just that I had to be the older sister, do the right thing, but to hear Nikos say those words has my knees softening.

I forget about everything but this dangerous man who's kissing me again, so passionately, I push closer against him. His fingers slide along my drenched core, and he growls in a possessive way that tells me he wants so much more.

"Your adorable kiss, your wet pussy, melt my heart," he says between our kisses. Then he pushes a finger into me, and I moan, realizing how starved I am for his touch. His mouth is on mine with the kind of passion that makes my skin tingle with electricity. Everything about him has me floating, with all my problems falling away.

When he pushes another finger into me, my world explodes. I clutch onto his shirt, holding myself up, and I'm completely lost to him.

"Do you want this now?" he asks.

I moan my answer, "Yes."

But the grunt that comes from behind us distracts me, rudely interrupting us. Nikos pulls away instantly, and he turns to find Crius standing at the corner of the tavern. It reminds me of him watching Ragnar and me in the woods, and now I'm with Nikos.

Heat sears my insides, and I lower my head, my cheeks burning. What does he think of me? That I screw any man who shows me attention? I shouldn't care, but for some reason, I do.

I'm rushing past Nikos before I know it, and right by Crius, not able to look at him.

In haste, I button up my pants and fix the shirt underneath my vest, while cursing myself.

What the hell are you doing?

I push open the swinging tavern door and instantly spot Ragnar and Stone near the window at a round table already filled with plates of food and glasses of beer.

The room is mostly made up of men, with a few females who look like the kind you hire by the hour.

Men look at me as if I'm the new entertainment, but when Ragnar stands up and whistles, the whole room looks his way.

"She's with me, so keep your eyes to yourself before I rip them out," he growls.

Biting my lip, I hurry across the room while my heart is pounding at his possessiveness. I know the men keep telling me Ragnar shares everything with them, but the way he's staring at me right now leaves me wondering if he'd tear apart Nikos if he saw what Crius had.

8

"Perfect timing, asshole," I rasp at Crius as I march toward him while he stands at the corner of the tavern. Because of his interruption, Narah bolted from my arms just when I had been ready to fuck her and make her mine.

Now, I'm left outside with Crius, his gaze sharpening at my words. Yet he doesn't bat an eye at the three dead dudes, but then again, I've seen him take out a man for simply looking at him wrong.

"I never said to stop." His lips curl up with his smirk. "I was rather enjoying the show, though it would be better if I wasn't staring at your ugly, naked ass the whole time. But not sure how Ragnar would feel about you pulling that shit with his girl, but you know, you do you."

I pause in front of him, my teeth clenching, and I am dying to smash my fist into his smug face for pissing me off. On the bright side, he's not losing control of his wolf, but he's being his usual sarcastic prick.

"What the fuck, man? We share. That has always been the agreement." Honestly, I'm not certain why I even care. If he wants her for himself, I shouldn't give a rat's ass, but for some goddamn reason, I do.

No female has ever called to me like she does, so I can't deny the rise she gets out of me. All I can think about is pinning her against the wall and taking her savagely, making sure she'll never forget the way I fuck her. How I won't stop until I break her and she begs for more. Her vulnerable edge nearly destroys me, and each time she blushes around me, my cock hardens. So what the hell am I supposed to do with that?

I've just finished drowning in her softness, in her sugary, sex-filled scent. Somehow, I managed some semblance of control around her, or I would already be balls deep inside her, so that's a miracle in itself.

But my desire for her isn't the biggest issue here, now is it? And neither is Ragnar's feral possessiveness over her. I've seen the way he looks at her, too. The issue is that I'm not the only one who wants her. Especially when just watching her is hypnotic, the way she walks with her hips swaying, how she tilts her head whenever she's talking to you like she's utterly absorbed in the conversation. The girl's completely oblivious to the impact she has on those around her.

"Don't know what to say, bruh, but you see the way Ragnar is with her." Crius shrugs nonchalantly like he doesn't give a shit. What a liar. "He's already fucked her twice, bitten her, marked her. Never seen him do that before with another Omega. There's something about her, so just saying, don't get your hopes up that he'll share this one." He almost sounds like he's looking out for me. Crius might be a dickhead, but he has his caring moments.

But going back to his words, I knew Ragnar took her a second time, but I won't lie, it stings like a bitch after I kissed her. Especially after groping the softness of her breast, remembering the way she clutched onto me, making those delicious moaning sounds. She's the kind of woman who brings men like me to their knees, and my blood pumps ferociously to my dick as I picture her wet pussy... if only I got the chance before knuckle-head here interrupted us.

"Are you trying to convince me or yourself?" I snarl in response and walk past him, my wolf still roaring inside me, my lust for her slaughtering me. But I have the willpower to ride this through, because I don't have another choice.

I look down at myself, completely nude and splattered in blood. My concern isn't the nudity in front of others, not when it's second nature for wolves, but more that the blood might be a dead giveaway that I murdered those guys. Not sure Ragnar will appreciate us being attacked during our celebration feast for the dead.

I march right past the tavern and into the inn where our stuff is. By the time I re-emerge, dressed in new clothes and clean of blood, I'd come up with an answer to dealing with Narah. Marking her might be out of the question for now, but that doesn't mean I can't enjoy teasing her, making her blush, and having her come to me. Who says going down on her isn't possible? That's not exactly claiming a girl. And I'm fucking aching to taste her, to have her sit on my face. Then, it's her choice, really. It's not like I can deny the adorable little thing if she begs me for more.

With a grin, I shove the door open and march inside the tavern.

The smell of beer and roasting meats hits me instantly, followed by a pungent perspiration from too many fucking men. The joint is full of Alphas and Betas, most paying attention to half a dozen females serving meals and flirting with them. A red-haired woman in a black slinky dress stands on a small stage, belting out a heartfelt song, which is mostly drowned out by the raucous laughter and voices.

I cross the busy room, swerving around packed tables, and reach ours near the window. I flop down in the empty seat.

Narah sits next to Ragnar. They're all staring at me, except Narah. She has her head low and is stabbing her fork into a roasted potato. She's wearing black gloves to cover her magic-stained fingers because the Neanderthals in this part of the world fear magic instead of embracing it.

Look at us sharing a meal like one happy-go-lucky family.

"What'd you change clothes for?" Stone asks me, always the inquisitive bastard sticking his nose where it doesn't belong. He's Ragnar's cousin and the reserved one of the bunch. Crius gives him a lot of shit, but I'm starting to realize it's his form of showing affection. Crius is damn loyal to the pack and us four, and while Stone is the same, he is also a terrifying fighter especially when he wields his elemental magic. I glance at the ink of his runes that peek out over his collarbone and neck from under his shirt. I remember him once telling me it was a custom that came down from his mother's family to be inked with them at the age of five, even if his father loathed them.

We're an odd group who all have major father issues. Maybe that's the reason we all work so well together, especially under Ragnar's command. He always puts his pack first, unlike our own fathers.

I look over at Stone, who's watching me. Right, he's waiting for a response. So, I give him a lame one. "Why are you obsessed with what I'm wearing?" I answer and reach over to fill my plate with slices of beef brisket, roasted vegetables, and toasted bread smothered in butter. My mouth's salivating.

"It's just a question." He pushes the point, then takes a long drink from his glass of beer.

"I think he wants to see you naked," Crius stage whispers to me, chuckling. "I mean, I don't get it, Stone. Have you seen Nikos' ass? It's nasty."

Narah half-chuckles, glancing up, looking at me through her long lashes, and I'm not sure if I should take her response as an insult, or maybe she's a lot more laid back than I think.

Plus, I appreciate Crius derailing the conversation. He knows Stone as well as me, who's like a dog with a bone when something's got him curious.

Stone gulps down the rest of his deep brown beer and sets the glass on the table, already eyeing the server girl for a refill. "His ass is the last thing I want."

Crius howls into laughter, slamming a hand to the table, making everything on it jump, which has Ragnar shaking his head as he digs into his meal. "I get it. You want cock."

"Just fuck off, both of you," I answer, unable to stop smiling at our usual table conversations, revolving around cocks and getting laid... we just haven't progressed to the latter topic yet. And I'm guessing we won't with Narah in our company.

When the server arrives, she floods the table with more plates of assortments from pasta covered in molten cheese, baked salmon, hard cheeses, and a platter of fruit with nuts dipped in honey.

Narah is already helping herself to the green grapes, coated with the sweet bee nectar, and pops one into her mouth, then another, a drop of honey dripping from the corner of her mouth. Her tongue darts out quickly and licks it up. I'm utterly mesmerized. It's clear I pay way too much attention to this girl.

But I'd have to be a eunuch to not notice such beauty.

Everyone's gone quiet at the table, as I'm not the only one watching the way she's eating the grapes, her lips pressed around each one before sucking it into her mouth. I won't lie, my cock is twitching at the image. And in my mind, I'm suddenly back with her outside, squeezing her breast, drawing her tongue against mine, and inhaling the scent that is all sex.

I'm craving to slide my fingers into her pants and her drenched core, teasing her clit as I make her scream, as she looks at me with those amber eyes. She wants to say no, but can't help herself and pleads for more. I'm desperate to see the honey seeping from her pussy after I bring her to climax, again and again.

My heart is racing, and I shift in my chair uncomfortably.

Goddammit.

She's killing me, and I pull my attention away from her and back to my food. All I'm doing is giving myself a hard-on and blue balls with such thoughts. Still, I can't help but smirk at how close I came and how I'll make her mine one way or another.

Ragnar has his hand under the table, and it's clear he's stroking her thigh. She's smiling up at him with the same look she gave me outside. Fire flares in my chest, but I also know my place and need to pull back before I leap over the table and lose control.

The thing about Omegas is that no matter how hard an Alpha resists, we're biologically drawn to them, so these emotions driving me mad are nature's way of ensuring our race continues, that we rut and make babies. But the part I find curious is the strength of allure I feel for her when she's not even in heat or my fated mate.

I'm worried for her if she ever does go into heat around us because I have no idea how we'll be able to hold back without us killing each other to get to her.

It's why many females aren't seen around. Many are claimed before their heat hits, especially when they meet their fated mate.

It was one reason Ragnar's sister was sent to my pack. Her heat made her ready, and that also made her a wanted asset. Like me, we were both pawns to be traded. According to my father, that would be like hitting two birds with one stone.

"You leave today, Nikos," Father commands from the doorway of my chamber, his shoulders broad, his deep chestnut hair pulled back off his brutally scarred face. His green eyes narrow against the morning sun's rays drenching my room. Mother tells me they are just like mine, but I refuse to believe I share anything with the man who once told me his offspring were nothing but pawns to be used to grow his strength. And that one day, I'll make him proud when my time comes.

I'm on my feet, putting down the book I'd been reading on historic warfare by a tribe called Samurai. "What mission am I to complete this time?"

Since I could walk, I've been training in warfare, so he uses me on missions, which I suspect are mostly to do with getting me out of his way.

His lips thin and turn upward, the conniving expression on his face suddenly worrying me. He never smiles at me, and when he does, it comes with pain at my expense. Last time he looked at me this way, I traveled across the country to spy on a new encroaching pack, only to find myself in the middle of a savage territory war that had shit to do with me. I ended up with two broken ribs and a cracked skull. When I returned home, Father's only response had been, "I hear you fell in battle. What good are you to me?"

But I accepted long ago to live with his cruelty, as have my two older brothers.

"A mission of utmost importance," he answers. "I've found a bride for your brother, Anker, and with it comes peace from the brute Ulv Wolves who are on our doorsteps. We lose warriors daily to war on both sides."

I wait for my role in his latest scheme to become clear.

But before he responds, several of his guards charge into the room and seize me by the arms. I shove against them, my pulse racing. "What the hell's going on?"

Father strolls into my room, his hands resting across his round belly. "I've struck a deal with the Alpha of Ulv Wolves. To create peace between our packs, he will send us his only daughter, and you will be the exchange from our pack."

My stomach hardens. "Fuck no! I won't do this." My thoughts fly to my mother left with him, to Eve, the girl I gave my promise to marry when she came into her heat, which should be soon. She's fifteen, and I'm twenty-one. I've adored her for so long that I don't care if she's my fated mate or not. She's mine.

I thrash against the guards' iron grips. "Release me," I growl.

But Father steps up to me and grabs my hair, fisting it, forcing my head to the side, giving me a sickening smile. "Listen here, you little shit. Blood bleeds into our rivers from all the dead, and your life has finally received purpose from the gods. You will go to the enemy and learn to love them, suck their cocks for all I care, but you make it fucking work as your presence ceases our war."

A deep rumble rolls inside me. "You sonofabitch!" My heart is pounding, and I shake with fury.

Father releases me. "You ever set foot in my home again and I will kill you myself. You are no longer a Balor wolf. Now *make me proud," he mocks. With a wave of his hand, the guards haul my ass out of my family home.*

I shove against them fiercely when a sharp jab strikes the back of my neck. My world spins suddenly, and my knees hit the ground. Everything's a blur, and the last person I see is my mother, crying, calling for me as I'm whisked away.

That was over three years ago, when my life grew so dim I've never found my light again, and the wound in my soul is still as fresh as if Father's rejection just happened.

I swallow a mouthful of food when a shadow falls over our table. It silences Stone's constant chatter, and I glance up to the barkeeper, wiping his hands on his short apron. "The man you've been waiting for has arrived." He glances over at a guy striding across the tavern. He looks to be in his forties, has a handlebar mustache, and wears a checkered shirt and slacks.

"Thank you," Ragnar says and shakes the man's hand, sliding into his palm a silver coin for payment.

When the barkeeper retreats with a huge grin, Stone and Crius march toward the poor sucker who has no clue what's coming his way. I finish the rest of my beer when Ragnar catches my eye. He gives me a knowing nod, one that states we don't let the man walk away until we get what we need out of him. "Do what it takes," he instructs, then turns to Narah. "Let's leave."

She frowns. "What? No, I have to find out."

Ragnar's on his feet and grabs her by the arm, forcing her out of her chair. "I'll carry you if I have to. We'll find out soon enough, but in case things get out of hand, I don't want you in the thick of it."

Despite her protests, he hauls her out of the tavern. I do adore her feistiness.

When I glance back around, Stone and Crius are practically carrying the guy toward me. His face is panic-stricken, and instantly I know this will be an easy job. He also came in alone, so I doubt he has buddies who'll jump in to fight for him.

I scan the room regardless, just in case.

Crius shoves the guy toward our table, and I kick out an empty chair. "Sit," I instruct.

He slides into the seat quickly, his face pale and eyes widening with that panicked look as he frantically turns his attention from me to Stone and Crius.

"What's this about?" he asks with a shaky voice. "I want no trouble."

"And you'll have none if you answer our questions," I say, taking the steak knife from the table and start spinning it over my fingers. More for effect, but if he pisses me off, he may lose a finger or two.

He sees me staring at his hand and bunches them in his lap. "Please, I never knew the sheep belonged to you, or I never would have taken it."

"Fuck man, we don't want to know about your weird-ass fetish," Crius growls, scrunching up his nose.

He's trembling before I can even grill him.

Stone is groaning. "Shit! He's pissed his pants."

I shuffle backward, not wanting to be near him. "Fucking hell. Okay, let's make this quick," I blurt. "Yesterday, six men left town with a female. And you spoke with them, correct?"

He nods. He's such a weasel-like man with a thin neck that can easily be snapped. "Yes, I-I bumped into them as I left the tavern. The girl looked scared and was crying, but one of the men had his hand over her mouth." He shrugs. "But really, what could I do? It was six against me, and it's not the first time females have been traded or taken, so I didn't think much of it."

I sigh because he's right. Women are commodities, but that doesn't mean I'll stand by and let assholes get away with it either.

The man's staring at me then glances down at the steak knife in my grasp. "I-if it was just one or two of them, I could have taken them on," he drones on, which are all lies. This guy's a runner, not a fighter.

"Stop shitting your pants, man," Crius says, sitting on his other side. "We don't need you to fight. Just tell us what the fuck they said. Names, anywhere they went. What the hell did they say that can help us find them?"

Stone sits across the table and is leaning forward, staring death into the poor man's soul.

"T-they told me to fuck off and shoved me out of the way. I didn't try to make conversation with them, but I did hear one name." He gasps for air, his chest pumping furiously for oxygen.

"And? What the fuck are you pausing for?" Stone snarls.

"M-Martell. One of them kept mentioning someone called Martell."

9

NARAH

"Martell." I choke out the name, and instantly my wolf shoves forward, moaning in my chest as if his name alone has awakened her longing. But I'm shaking with anger, and I glance at the four Vikings who've just given me a rundown of who took Jae. "That fucking cocksucker," I blurt, causing Crius to smirk and nod at my outburst. "I can't believe he took her."

But I also detest how quickly my wolf reacts to hearing his name.

Just saying it leaves a bitter taste in my mouth, and I think I'm going to hurl. He's my fated mate and the man who not only rejected me but threw me off a cliff. I hadn't even spent one night with him before he discovered my magic and abandoned me. Bastard.

All because wolves like me who carry magic are cursed.

We're hunted.

Hated.

Destroyed.

And I'm going to shove all that cursed bullshit right up his ass when I find him for stealing my sister. That piece of shit. I'm shaking with anger.

I glance over to the four Vikings in the room with me, knowing they are so different from other wolves in the Savage Sector, and part of me wonders how much that has to be a regional thing. Especially seeing as Stone and Crius carry some sort of magic of their own.

These emotions strangling me aren't like before, and I thank the moon for Ragnar's bite to tame my wolf's desperation over Martell. But still, the fact that a name alone has her stirring worries me. How will she react when I cross paths with him?

I refuse to be weak for him again. To let my body betray me over a man who tried to murder me. I will get my sister back and make him pay. To get my revenge because if he's found me, he'll never stop until he gets what he wants... my death. Because I may be many things, but I'm no fool. As much as that bastard hates me, his wolf will be pining after me too. That's why he needs to find me. Eliminate the problem, and his wolf will get over me, which leaves my sisters vulnerable. I should fear him, but I'm too angry that he's found us.

"I need to go after her right now!" My hands are shaking badly.

"Are you sure about this?" Ragnar asks me. "Traveling in the dark can be dangerous."

Every inch of me is trembling, not because of his words, but that the longer I do nothing, the farther my sister gets from me while in the company of the devil.

"I'm not backing down. You can come with me or stay here, but I'm going. Nikos said they were on foot, so if we're on horses, we should catch up to them, right?"

He rubs his hand across the short stubble across his jawline. "Depends on whether they found transportation, and if they stayed on the same road. But I'm ready to spill blood if you are."

I tilt my head back, meeting his gaze. The man is panty-melting gorgeous, and he's proven it twice, which can distract me horribly. But to hear the determination in his voice, to know I'm not alone, fills me with confidence.

"I love your tenacity, Narah," Crius adds, drawing my attention from Ragnar. "Maybe you can send some over to me. Maybe with a kiss, just like you—"

"Thanks for the compliment, but you definitely are not lacking tenacity," I reply, instantly stealing the rest of his words while my heart hammers louder in my chest. Who would have thought that Crius is such a blabbermouth. But maybe he's told the other two about Nikos and me in the back of the tavern. It doesn't stop the heat crawling up my neck at what Ragnar might think.

Even Stone, who hasn't said a word and stands as still as a statue, studies me like he knows all my dirty secrets, which has me blushing even more.

"She has you there," Ragnar mutters, his voice dark, his attention focused on the window.

Crius runs his fingers down the two plaits of his brown beard, smirking. "Fine, but just so we make it clear. I will fucking bury every single asshole involved in Jae's kidnapping. Your sister's actually decent."

"No one's arguing with you on that point," Stone states.

"I'm just putting it out in the universe before one of your bastards steals my kills."

I snort a laugh at what he's worried about. "As long as I get Jae back in one piece, I don't care who kills them, but I want that bastard, Martell, sliced from throat to groin."

"Oh fuck me, but that's that hottest thing you've ever said." Crius groans, his hand slides down his body and gropes his cock over his pants.

Such a sexy animal, and I can't help but be turned on by him. I have every belief that he's rough in the bedroom, dominating, and rather large by the size of the package he's groping. In truth, I think that about all three of them... big bastards who could easily pin me down and have their way with me. Ragnar's already conquered me, and I can't even say it will never happen again. I know that if he comes for me, I'll melt.

But my head is pounding with worry for Jae, so I straighten my shoulders. "Are we doing this or not?"

"Fine," Ragnar finally answers. "I'll go down and find us some horses. The tavern owner was talking about someone who has a farm nearby. Stone, you're with me."

"I'm coming too if you're going to the tavern," Crius adds. "I'm fucking thirsty."

"Nikos, Narah?" Ragnar asks, an eyebrow arching ever so slightly in my direction.

"I'll wait here," I answer, standing near the bed, not in the mood to be surrounded by loud noises. When I'm so tense, I feel like I'm going to burst out crying any moment now.

"That makes two of us," Nikos responds, gaining a tight grin and nod from Ragnar, and the three of them walk out of the room, shutting the door behind them.

"Looks like it's just the two of us," he murmurs.

I look over at Nikos, the Viking who tempted me behind the tavern, and realize that maybe us being alone isn't such a good thing. He strolls across the room, his chestnut hair long and tied into one big dreadlock hanging down past his shoulders, the sides of his head shaved. His skin is tanned like he's spent his entire life outdoors. He's wearing dark jeans that perfectly fit him, following the curve of that scorching hot ass. Even in a simple, long-sleeved V-neck shirt, he's absolutely captivating. He's a giant. His hands could easily touch the ceiling if he reached up, especially next to me, but that just draws me to him even more.

He flops down on a chair at the table by the window. The faint light overhead flickers like it might go out. I doubt the generators to run this inn are sturdy enough to keep the rooms lit while the tavern blares with light.

"Sit down," he says and pushes out a seat for me with his foot.

He's leaning forward with his folded arms on the table, and they're huge too. There's something extremely sexy about strong forearms. Maybe it's knowing he can hold me in them and I'll feel safe. He has his eyes locked on me, watching my every move as I step closer. But there's something dancing behind them tonight like I'm the deer and he's the starved wolf studying his prey.

Makes me wonder why he decided to be the babysitter tonight...Does it have anything to do with our kiss behind the tavern?

Everything about Nikos is striking, especially when he looks at me as if I'm his meal.

I slide into the chair and pull my knees up, hugging them to my chest. "Do you think Jae will be okay?"

He loses that seductive look, his face taking on a serious expression. "If they wanted to hurt her, they would have done it in town instead of kidnapping her. Means they are taking her to someone or intend to use her for leverage."

Feeling sorry for myself, for Jae, I just sigh and prop my chin onto my knees. "It's me Martell wants, but he took my sister to ensure he gets that." He'll go to any length to get me back, to kill me, to put a stop to his wolf's agony. I should have known this would be the case, but I'd been too busy drowning myself. Plus, I tried hard to push him out of my thoughts for my wolf's sake.

Gold flecks glint in Nikos' green eyes, and I close mine, wanting the sting in my chest for Jae to end. He takes my hand and drags me off my seat, my eyes flying open. I stand in front of him as he remains seated, my ass propped up against the table.

"I'm going to do you a favor," he mutters, his hands on my hips, keeping me in place, his thumbs finding the bare skin peeking out from under my vest.

"Is that so?" I can't help but smile, even though part of me wants to cry that things keep going badly for me.

"Before every fight and hunt, we are taught to find peace with our inner demons. So that when you step into battle, there is nothing to distract you, only the primal rage you hold toward your enemy."

"So, what do you do to clear your mind? Meditate? Train?"

"Find a girl and fuck her brains out."

I might have just gasped, as that isn't the response I expected.

He's smiling, the corners of his eyes crinkling, seeming to love the reaction that drew from me.

"Well, I guess that's one way of doing it. Can't say I've ever tried that, but I can see how it makes you forget everything." I'm rambling and hot all of a sudden under Nikos' attention.

"We started something behind the tavern, and I want more. I want to be with you, Narah. It's that simple."

I struggle for a moment to respond, as my mind is still caught on his earlier words. Finally, I find my voice, saying, "Nothing is ever simple, you know that. And it sounds complicated to me."

He pulls me toward him to stand between his legs, his large hands grasping my hips, and he's eye-level with my chin, his gaze on my lips. "Only if you make it so."

My breathing quickens a little. He might be onto something because I'm completely lost when I'm near him. Captivated by the way his fingers slide across my back under my vest and shirt.

"I want to give you something that I know will help," he breathes the words, leaning closer, his mouth on my neck.

I tremble, unable to move. "And you'll get something out of it too, I suppose."

"Of course. I want to know if your pussy tastes as sweet as your honeyed scent." He presses his face into the curve of my neck, inhaling, his hands flat against my back, pressing me tightly against him. My breasts brush up against his collarbones, and I'm hyper-aware of every touch, every breath he draws.

How am I supposed to respond to such a comment that has me burning up and ignites a fire between my thighs; to have this powerful Viking be so straightforward with what he craves?

His mouth moves to the base of my ear, his lips sending tingles all over my body. I lean further against him, my body betraying me as a shiver of excitement races down my spine and right to my core, where my nerves are pulsing.

"Is this what you want?" he asks.

"I-I…"

His tongue curls my earlobe into his mouth. It's so warm. He sucks on it tenderly, taking small nips, and his lips are like fire. My legs shake while my fingers grip his shoulders, holding on because I am certain if he lets me go now, I'll fall.

"Is that a yes?" he practically purrs in my ear. "Do you want me to taste you and tell you how sweet you are?"

His fingers fumble with the buttons of my pants, and I do nothing to stop him.

My face must be bright red by now, but I need this in my life. "Ah-aha," I stammer, and that has him pushing my pants and underwear all the way down my legs. I step out of them, toeing my shoes off at the same time as the coolness of the room finds my skin, and it takes everything to not cover myself.

"It would be rather rude on your part to make a promise and not fulfill it," I manage to say with a confidence I know comes from the arousal flaring through me.

But to stand half-naked in front of this god has me quivering, and my bravery fades fast. Nikos gets on his feet, and near him, I realize just how tiny I am in comparison. It's crazy how that turns me on so madly.

"Narah, babe," he says, unraveling the cord from my vest, undoing it quickly, then lifting my shirt up and over my head. "I need to see all of you. It's driving me fucking insane with need."

My hands instantly cover myself, but he's pulling my arms away from across my chest. "No hiding. You are too beautiful to ever hide your body from me." His strong hands grip my hips, and I'm suddenly sitting on the table.

His mouth is on my neck again as he nudges my legs open with his hand and steps closer. He cages me in with his body.

I tremble, and he cups the sides of my face, drawing me to him, and I kiss him desperately. My mouth crashes against him, and he kisses me back with a bruising hunger, tugging on my breasts. His hand is on my throat, and he guides me back onto the table, ripping from our kiss, fire flaring in his gaze.

He sits on the chair in front of me. I try to close my legs, but he's making a tsking sound as he pries them open. "Don't think about it. Now that I've seen your perfect cunt, you are mine."

Before I can even try to come up with something to say, his mouth is on my inner thigh, and I tense, completely forgetting how to talk. "Just look how pretty you are."

His eyes are not on my face but my pussy. And he gently places a kiss on my lips down there, then runs a tongue up my slit.

I moan. The feel of his mouth on me is the most incredible sensation in the world. I'm buzzing all over, and nothing is as good as having a powerful man lick me.

He widens my thighs, his fingers peeling apart my lips, and pushes his face deeper. His lips and tongue do things to me that have me crying out and my back arching. I grip the sides of the table and hold on tight.

"You are so much sweeter than honey. You are delicious."

I crane my neck up, but he's buried his face between my thighs again, his eyes on mine as he smothers himself with my drenched wetness. He tugs at my lips and licks me wildly.

My cries morph into screams with how quickly he devours me, with the orgasm already racing through me.

"Nikos, I don't think I can..." Arousal bursts through me, and I'm bowed backward on the table, howling the orgasm that tears through me. He doesn't stop and licks me ferociously like he can't get enough of tasting me.

I yell out his name, writhing, my body convulsing, coming hard in his mouth. He's licking everything up, from my pussy to what runs down my inner thighs.

Gasping for breath, I collapse back on the table, smiling, loving how good I feel. And how I want more and more.

"You taste even better than I imagined." He licks the cum from his lips, his chin and nose glistening as he looks up at me. "You are the most beautiful creature I've ever seen, and to claim you is everything to me."

He yanks his shirt off, revealing a wall of muscles, inked tribal patterns run over his bulging biceps. Then tears open the buttons on his pants and drops them. When he stands, I might have gaped at the size of him. Ragnar is very well built, but Nikos' cock... I don't think I can breathe.

"I'm going to fuck you now," he informs me, taking my hand and drawing me up and off the table.

"I-I don't think that's going to fit," I murmur, my heartbeat picking up again, being completely serious.

"It will be fine. I give you my word." He suddenly spins me by my waist to face away from him, then bends me over the table. His strong hands grip my hips as his foot parts my legs. "Open up for me. I'm barely keeping it together. I need to fuck you, to be inside your sweet cunt."

"I never expected you to be so... big," I exclaim.

He chuckles. "Why, thank you, gorgeous." And he enters me swiftly.

I tense while he plunges deeper into me, somehow stretching me wide enough to fit.

My breaths are raspy, and I moan at having something so huge inside me.

His hands are on my ass, squeezing, then he slowly pulls out and pushes in again, but it doesn't last. He's pounding into me so fast that I lose my breath. The friction of our union sends me into panting shudders. The raging heat between us increases rapidly, matching Nikos' thrusting tempo.

He rides me.

My eyes shut, and I'm lost to everything but this moment in time. I begin to quake, low growls rubbing over my throat as he fucks me savagely. And I could swear he's getting bigger inside me, the pressure within me building. He's about to knot, I sense it, the weight of him is incredible.

When he reaches his hand around to my hip to my pussy, my hips give a small jerk. "Come for me, suck down on my cock." With two fingers, he pinches my clit, hard.

I can barely breathe as he violently thrusts into me, making me dizzy. His thunderous growl booms around us, and with the way he grips my ass and his fingers teasing my pussy, I come completely undone for a second time.

I throw my head back, crying out as the orgasm rattles me. While Nikos' huge erection pulses, spilling his seed into me. My climax rocks me to the core. He's tense against me, growling, his cock knotting inside me, expanding against my inner walls to a super snug fit.

Clenching my teeth tight, I float down and worry I might break a tooth with the intensity of that second orgasm.

Nikos swoops me into his arms and lifts me from the table, both of us still connected, and walks us to the bed.

"That was fucking amazing," he moans, followed by a savage growl from his chest where his wolf makes himself very well known.

We fall onto the bed, him deeply embedded in me, his arms wrapped around me as he spoons me.

This is where I feel safe...in his arms.

My chest is light for once, the overbearing weight of all my problems has left me...for now, at least. I twist my head around to see his eyes are still hazy, and I know he's still pumping into me. Alphas produce a ridiculous amount of seed.

He smiles, his grip tightening. "I wish I could sweep you away from this world and find a place where no one could ever hurt you again."

10

NARAH

It's late, the night air sticky, and the heavy moon glows brightly beside the storm clouds.

After the earth-shattering time with Nikos, I'll never forget, I must have fallen asleep because I woke up to find my belongings packed and fresh clothes waiting for me by the bed. I was alone in my room, Nikos gone. From the window, I'd seen Crius down in the street with Ragnar waiting in front of the inn, so I made a mad rush to join them with my belongings. Apparently, they had to wait for horses to be brought from the local farm, which is what took so long. And now Stone and Nikos are collecting the horses from the back of the tavern. I'm still blushing from what Nikos and I did, and I have no idea if Ragnar and the others know.

I feel amazing, but don't want to discuss any of it with the rest of the guys.

I push the strap of my pack higher on my shoulder and lick my dry lips as I stare at the lights beaming from the tavern windows. Laughter and music pour out of the place. During the weeks I've lived here, waiting to find my sisters, the tavern served beer and food, any time of the day or night.

A clopping sound of hooves striking stone comes from my right, and I turn my head. Halfway down the street, Nikos is guiding two horses on either side of him by the reins, and Stone has two behind him. Dark beasts who neigh as if they've been woken up.

I frown at the sight, seeing as I'm a complete virgin when it comes to riding a horse.

But I don't see anyone bringing a fifth horse, which I'm secretly happy about. But getting to my sister supersedes the dread of being thrown and trampled by one of the huge beasts.

"You're riding with me." Ragnar has his arm around my back before he collects my bag.

"Okay," I answer as I watch a huge chestnut mare step up in front of us, shaking her head and scratching the ground with her front hoof. Each guy gravitates to a horse, with Ragnar tossing my bag to Stone to carry as his luggage.

In seconds, Ragnar mounts the horse, straddling her back, and is settled in the saddle. There's a thick blanket behind him, which will be my seat, I guess. Looks easy enough, though the animal is a lot taller than me. Next to the horse, I might as well be a dwarf.

Ragnar offers me his hand. "Put your foot in the stirrup, and I'll pull you up."

I don't hesitate, as I prefer he doesn't know the horse makes me slightly queasy because of her sheer size.

Gingerly, I place my hand in his, then lift my foot to the stirrup. His grip tightens, and I'm suddenly flying up and toward him.

"Whoa." A sliver of panic strikes as I frantically reach for Ragnar. I crash right into him as I swing my leg over the horse.

My ass hits the blanket behind Ragnar, and I clutch onto the back of his coat with a death grip. "Geez, it's really high up here, isn't it?" I gasp, quickly wrapping my arms around his waist.

He laughs at me and pats my hand. "I'll keep you safe."

The five of us are all geared up, and Ragnar nudges our horse forward. My body sways, and it seriously feels like I'm going to slip off this beast any second now. I'm tense, holding on for dear life.

Nikos, the second in command, takes the lead, followed by us, then Stone at our side and Crius at our rear.

If I wasn't freaking out about falling, I might think there's something almost comforting about traveling with these four powerful Alphas. Their protection is undeniably attractive. These aren't things I should be thinking when we have a group of assholes to find, but I can't deny how much my feelings for these Vikings are growing.

We pick up the pace once we reach the edge of town, and my heart thumps harder as my body bumps and slides against Ragnar's back, whether I want it to or not.

My arms remain locked around Ragnar's middle, my body plastered to him, and there is absolutely no way to stop myself from rubbing my breasts all over him on our ride.

"First time on a horse?" he asks, turning his head to look back at me, his eyebrow arching up an inch.

"That obvious?"

"You're strangling the hell out of my stomach, but if it makes you feel safe, I'll suffer through it," he says sarcastically.

"Oh, sorry." I slightly loosen my hold from around his waist, but I'm not letting go completely. Instead, I fist his coat to hold onto something. My hands are sweating like crazy, not to mention my legs shaking from squeezing so hard to stay on the horse.

He laughs louder, and I do love the way he sounds when he's happy... So at least there's that.

"If it's too much for you, Ragnar, I'll gladly take her on my horse," Stone interrupts. "You can strangle the life out of any part of me, babe, if it means rubbing your tits all over me."

I almost choke on my next breath and roll my eyes. "Of course, you will," I jokingly say.

"If Stone gets her, then it's only fair we take turns carrying her," Crius pipes up from the rear. Nikos jumps in too with, "I'm down with that."

Ragnar doesn't say yes or no to their offers, so I reply, "Not sure any of you can do it as well as Ragnar." And the moment my words register, the three guys begin laughing.

"I mean, the way he's riding the horse with me," I correct myself.

Crius is howling crazily now, one hand clutching his stomach, and I'm shaking my head. "Oh, he'd definitely want to ride you again."

My cheeks are on fire.

"Though Nikos was pretty close too, seeing he had his hand down your pants earlier," he continues, and I want to die. But this also tells me the others don't know yet what we did up in the room. Please let it stay that way. I'm not that comfortable talking openly about my sexual escapades, considering Ragnar had been my first.

"You literally suck balls," I snap at Crius, who coughs a chuckle.

"When did this happen?" Stone asks, his eyebrows drawing together. "Why do I always miss out on all the fun?"

"No balls for me, beautiful," Crius utters, smirking. "Only your sweet pussy, if you'll let me."

He grins at me. And yet the whole time, Ragnar has said nothing. I bury my face in his back, wishing I could be anywhere but here with these three asses.

"Ragnar," I begin my voice barely a whisper.

"It's okay, little fox. Nikos told me. Like I said before, there are no secrets between us."

He had? My stomach clenches hard. How much had he told him?

I notice the rest of the guys have fallen quiet, which tells me they are just as curious about what their leader has to say. It also means that Crius said all that shit on purpose to get Ragnar to speak.

And it seems we'll be waiting forever because he didn't take the bait and is not talking. I don't even know why I'm giving so much thought to this. What's the big deal? I slept with Ragnar twice, then with Nikos, desperately wanted to kiss Crius, and daydreamed about Stone. Not that I'm keeping count, but something must be wrong with me. My fated mate wants me dead, and I'm sleeping with dangerous Alphas who I've made a deal with.

I am losing it.

Men are dangerous, Mother would tell me.

And this is why I shouldn't be playing with fire. As much as my body and wolf seem to protest, what will happen after I get my sisters back? I'm not sure yet, but it worries me that these Vikings are about to start a war with all wolves in the Savage Sector. So, do I want to be in the middle of chaos with my sisters? And I don't even know the deal with my mother.

Refusing to think about that right now, I hold on.

I have no idea how long we've been riding; hours, feels like days, but my ass has never been this sore. The men are silent as we travel through the woodlands, following a wide trail, and the only light is the glow of a burning torch in Nikos' hand.

Trees bleed into the night, and I can barely make out the lofty pines on either side of us. There are no other sounds, only the striking of horse hooves against dirt.

A gravelly groan comes from behind us. It's loud enough that we've all heard it as each of us is glancing over our shoulder.

Nikos' light sweeps over the land, barely revealing three figures stumbling unevenly out of the woods and coming our way in their sluggish attempt at running. Their deathly groans have me gasping loudly.

"It's the undead," I murmur, my heart racing.

They're easier to see now as they come closer, in torn clothes, one with a missing eye, skeletal faces, and a woman with half her jaw hanging at an odd angle.

"Fuck!" Stone murmurs. "Let's get out of here."

"There's only three." Crius draws out his axe. "I vote we take the fuckers out."

"And how many more are in the woods that we can't see yet?" Nikos voices my exact concern.

"Fuck that," Crius groans. "I want to destroy something, and they look like fun things to smash."

"Sure thing, Hulk," Stone groans.

"Who the fuck is that?" Crius asks, climbing off his horse. I'm just as curious, what's a Hulk?

"Forget it. You don't read up on anything from the old times."

My eyes are glued on the creatures stumbling toward us rapidly. "Umm, can we please leave?"

"Crius," Ragnar's voice deepens. "We are not doing this now. Get back on the fucking horse."

Holy crap, the air just thickened in a split second.

Crius holds Ragnar's stare for a long moment , not seeming to care that the goddamn undead are coming toward us. Maybe that's his intention, but not mine. I need to be as far from them as possible before I scream and run away like a mad person.

His gaze breaks from Ragnar's, and he leaps back into his saddle. We are off again, the five of us rushing out of there with incredible speed. I'm latched to Ragnar's back, holding on for dear life as I'm jostled about on the galloping horse.

I keep looking back at the handful of additional undead spilling onto the trail. Fear pounds rapidly in my chest. If we had stayed a moment longer, we'd have been surrounded by them. I press closer to Ragnar, thankful he got us the heck out of there.

Wind blows through my hair, tugging on my clothes. Even when I look back, and there's no sight of the creatures, we don't stop. The thing about the undead is that they are relentless, needy things that will cross the freaking country of Romania if they think food is available. So, no matter how far we get, they will continue their pursuit, meaning the quicker we move, the more time we'll have to find my sister and escape before we're attacked.

The undead have never been this far north in Romania before but have plagued the south in the Shadowlands Sector, eating anything and everything that moves. I've heard stories of the enormous hordes that cross the lands, and the only way the wolves survived is by enclosing themselves within lofty walls. Jae had told me about the Ash pack living down there, doing just that, and how they live with the enemy right on their doorstep. The thought scares the hell out of me, but I truly admire those Ash wolves for living amid the dead.

So the fact that we've just seen a small group in these woods is terrifying. How long before the Savage Sector is overrun by them too?

The virus that eliminated civilization so long ago took most humans in Europe. And while normal wolves like us are not immune to the disease, there are wolf packs who are different, such as the X-Clan who are immune. Once we die, we become one of those monsters because we are carriers, so survival is so much more than just living another day. It's doing anything to not end up as one of the undead.

I sometimes wonder what life was like before the virus ravaged the world. Before it killed so many and created monsters. The books I've read show it to be such a magical place with everything you want at your finger-tips. Sometimes it's hard to believe that such a place could have existed, especially with how fast it fell.

When Ragnar finally slows our horse to a stop, I instinctively glance back, as does Crius. There's nothing following us that we can see, but that doesn't mean they're not there.

I quickly stare out past Ragnar to find Nikos looking back at us, pointing forward.

Ragnar gives a small nod, and Nikos climbs off his steed. Then he runs down the track ahead of us as silent as the night, vanishing in the dark.

"What's going on?" I whisper.

"He's picked up on something. We'll know what soon enough," he answers in a soft voice. His hand is on mine across his stomach, and he holds me.

No one moves or speaks after that. I draw in a deep breath through my mouth, hating how vulnerable I feel in the middle of the dark woods. We're standing still, with only the dying glow of Nikos' torch, which he'd thrown to the ground.

The wait drags, and the longer we wait, the more my skin pricks. I listen for any sounds, anything that might indicate the undead's approach.

When Ragnar suddenly stiffens, I flinch in my seat. I look out past him and see Nikos rushing out of the darkness, moving as fast as a shadow, not making a sound.

He pauses near our horse, and Ragnar leans low to hear his words. My ears are pricked.

"Found them. They're heading along the valley, sticking to the river's edge. There are only two with Jae. The other four must be sweeping the woods on either side of them to ensure it's clear for their travel."

I might have made a small gasping sound. We found them!

"How far from our position?" Ragnar asks.

"Sixty yards tops. We ride up a bit further than ditch the horses."

Jae! Just hearing that Nikos found her has me eager to jump off the horse and run to her. But, of course, that would be a terrible idea.

"I'm ready," I whisper, butting in on their conversation.

"You heard, Narah. Take the lead," Ragnar instructs Nikos.

And in no time, we're riding forward in silence, my gaze constantly in front of us. I may not see much, especially now that Nikos has left the burning torch behind, but I'm trembling with anticipation.

It isn't long before we come to a stop.

Crius is off his horse in seconds, and he's helping me off mine just as fast, his hands on my hips, his breath on my ear. "Hey, gorgeous. Ready for your ex to gurgle his last breath?"

"Hell yeah."

He slides me down to my feet, and instantly an ache zaps along my thighs, my ass partly numb. I groan softly when I try to step. "Why does it hurt so much to ride a horse? I'm never going to walk straight again."

"That's what she said." Crius sniggers at his terrible joke.

Stone and Nikos are tying up the horses loosely to several trees, and Ragnar grabs my hand. "You're with me."

We run along the trail, me a bit more awkward from how sore I am, when I hear rushing water. We pause at the treeline, and a small clearing reveals the pebbly bank dipping into a river. I stick my head out with the guys, looking to our left, and there, in the distance, a light bops across the river's edge. I can barely make out three figures, but one is definitely shorter than the others.

My heart soars. *Jae. I'm coming.*

Ragnar pulls back, as do I. "Crius, cross the river and track us from that side. Nikos, you do this side. Anyone you find, kill them. Stone, you keep Narah close. Shit goes sideways, you get her the fuck away from here."

"Or, I just zap them," I suggest, raising my hands, but no one is smiling or agreeing.

Instead, Ragnar's gaze narrows down on me, his expression serious. "Can you control the power to not accidentally zap one of us or burn down the whole forest?"

"Well…" I shrug my shoulders. Shit, I hate that he's got a point.

"That's what I thought. Everyone knows the plan. We go now!"

I don't push the issue because he's correct. They've seen enough to know my power is uncontrollable, and I hate that I'm seen as the weak one, but at the end of the day, we are saving Jae. So I'm not going to complain about how we do this.

Crius and Nikos vanish into the night, our silent protectors, to get rid of Martell's men. He'd be with Jae, I have no doubt about that, and I curl my hands into fists.

Stone takes my hand, giving me a sweet smile. "Are you ready?"

"Yes. I want my sister back."

"Good," Ragnar responds. "Let's go." We rush forward, following the river's path from within the woods to avoid being seen.

I bite my lip, suddenly feeling all kinds of emotions. Fear, anxiety, excitement. But I'm struggling to shake off the feeding of dread curling in my gut that things will go sour. This is Martell we're dealing with, after all.

My wolf pours out of me, bones cracking, skin splitting, while my heart is pounding with adrenaline. It's been too long since I've had a decent hunt. Back home in Denmark, Ragnar, Stone, and I would head out into the wilderness at least twice a week to bring back big game for the family feasts, but sometimes we just hunted down rogue wolves. Cleaned out the woods of the beasts who attacked the locals, stole females, rutted and killed them. I miss hearing the last whimpers in their throats before I choked the life out of them.

It's surprisingly rewarding knowing that I'm doing a good deed for the pack. Hunting is the only time I truly feel at one with the Ulv pack after my father traded me to the enemy. It's why Ragnar and I have bonded so well, why my allegiance will only ever be to him. For him, I'll fight, I'll steal, I'll kill. Even if I still haven't worked out what I'll do with my future.

But for now, I can't think about what's coming, so I raise myself out of the shadows in my wolf form, then spring forward.

Each inhale I take picks up no wolf scents. The air is still tonight. Too fucking still, giving little away.

I glance toward the river and see I'm coming up close to Jae and the two men by her side. The two fuckers on this side of the river have to be somewhere nearby.

I suck in another deep breath, but still no scent. If I was protecting my Alpha in this situation, I'd be up front, ensuring there were no surprises. But that means an asshole is either behind me or very close.

Sliding in between two shrubs, I crouch. Sometimes, just watching and letting myself get in tune with the night is all I need. It's what we'd do while hunting. Choose a prime position and wait.

My eyes are adjusting, making it easier to see in the dark, and that's when I spot movement. It's small but enough to catch my attention.

I lick my lips and remain still.

A figure glides through the woods with almost no sound. He's in human form, which is a huge mistake on his part.

The second he passes me, I lunge out and slam into him unannounced. He hits the ground, face first, my weight on him.

I chomp down on the back of his neck, my teeth slicing flesh. The snap of bone is loud, considering everything's so silent. I do love the sound of breaking bones. The warmth of his wolf's blood drips down my chin.

He's shuddering, bucking, growling.

Save your breath... but on second thought, you won't need it for much longer.

I jerk my head sideways sharply and break his neck. That finality has him slumping beneath me. I let go and lick the blood from my lips, partly disappointed in how easy that was. I wanted a challenge.

Drawing away, I shake myself, needing to track down the other hunter.

But in the same moment I draw in a breath, something solid crashes into me. It comes so fucking fast, color me surprised, but when something stabs under my ribs, something so sharp that I'm stunned, panic flares.

The ache of a blade deep in me has me shuddering. I kick the bastard with my back legs with all the strength I have, a whimper spilling out of my throat from the burning pain spreading across my middle. Hastily, I angle my body away from him, so I'm facing him head-on. My rear is my weakness, but my teeth will destroy him.

Up on my feet, I stumble, and blood drips from the wound, but I stand tall because I've been injured before. It's not my first injury, and it won't be my last.

I lift my head to the fuckhead who's snarling under his breath, gripping the bloody knife in his hand. The world tilts, but I shake my head. I won't let him win.

"You killed my friend." He leans forward slightly. "And now it's your turn. Eye for an Eye, you piece of shit."

Lifting the blade, he comes at me as I lunge for him.

Crius

I stroll through the woods, resisting the urge to whistle. I badly want to do it right now because, let's be honest here, I want those dickheads in the woods to hear me, to come at me. Who the hell has time to hunt them down? We all know how it's going to end, so why should I exert extra energy I don't need to?

Of course, I make sure to stick as far from the river as possible to make noise. I'm not a complete moron.

My heavy steps crunch twigs and foliage, and as if on cue, two men emerge from the woods ahead of me.

I smile to myself. "Are you ready to play?"

They exchange looks, then grin my way.

"Oh, this is going to be fun. I can feel it in my bones." I'm going to make them cry so much for stealing Jae. She doesn't deserve whatever these pricks have in mind for her. And the fact that they caused Narah anguish is going to have them paying in blood.

The predictable duo rush at me. I sigh at how boring they are. I should have known things wouldn't go differently. But I'll suck it up.

I duck the first swinging fist, grab a thick branch off the ground, and launch it at the one guy's head. It hits with a dull thud, and he falls backward. Hopefully, he'll take a while to come back from that.

The second dude charges forward, his fist hitting me right in the nose. The sting radiating up to my eyes like a spider web of searing pain. "Fucking hell!"

He throws himself at me, slamming into me, catching me off guard. I stumble backward until my back slams into a tree. Shaking the pain from my head, I drive my fist at his kidney, having had enough of his snorting pig face in mine.

I kick him for good measure in the jewels too.

He's groaning and clutching his groin, while I retrieve the axe from my belt and spin it in my hand.

"My turn." Without hesitation, I swing it at the guy, the blade catching him right in the gut. "Ouch, that's gotta hurt."

He gurgles, dropping to his knees, spitting up blood. I shove a leg against his side as I tear my axe free. The man falls to his side, bleeding to death. He'll get no pity from me. The bastard deserved it for touching what doesn't belong to him.

The crack of a twig comes from right behind me. Instinct takes over, and I slam my elbow up and backward, catching the first guy right in the face.

He groans and stumbles back as I turn on him.

"You made a huge mistake coming here, and now it's time to pay the price, just like your buddy has." In my mind, all I can see is Narah and her tears when she found Jae had been kidnapped. Nothing can take away what she went through, but I'll try my fucking hardest.

The man is clutching his bleeding nose, eyes widening at seeing me approach with my axe. He's grappling to grab his knife from the sheath on his belt with his other hand.

"I'm going to kill you, you know," I tell him casually.

"Fuck you," he spits, his blade out in front of him, both hands now holding onto it, shaking ferociously.

"Really, if you're so fucking scared, why are you on this mission?" I tap the flat side of my axe to my chin. "Oh, I know because you have no spine and follow a weak-ass psychopath who's next on my hit list. Now, let's get this shit-show over with."

I need to do this fast because I want in on the action with Martell, the bastard who tried to kill Narah after rejecting her. Ragnar told us all. He holds no secrets from us. But I don't want Ragnar to steal all the fun now. I twirl the axe casually in my hand.

The man's eyes flick from the weapon to me. "Look, please, maybe we can talk about this." His pleas are just noise.

But in a flash, the bastard comes at me, bending low, his blade flashing in the moonlight. He moves fast, growling. My wolf surges forward, as does my anger. I swerve out of the way, missing the blade by an inch, but the thing catches my coat, tearing fabric.

"Bastard." Fury lunges through me, and my mind grows hazy. Madly, I swing at him, my axe swooping down, right into the side of his neck. Blood spurts out. With all my strength, I wrench it out and slam into him with the weapon, over and over, I don't see anything but the beautiful flow of red. My heart is pounding to a tune matched only by the crunch of bones beneath metal.

Now, this... this is me in my element.

Stone

I keep Ragnar in my sight as he slips through the shadows ahead of us. The man is a fucking warrior. I've seen him win so many battles at home, take down Alphas twice his size, and still his fucking asshole of a father refused to give him credit or promise him the throne to his pack. The dick told Ragnar he has to fight for the role with everyone else, and then he'd decide who the true champion will be to take the position.

Of course, that set Ragnar off and ended up with the pair in a physical fight. Not his finest moment, he confessed to me later, but family has a way of fucking you in the head.

The funny thing is that we all strive for their attention and affection, and yet they tend to be the ones who betray us the worst. My father, Ragnar's uncle, is just as cold-hearted, which is why, from a young age, I'd leave the house whenever I could to escape my dad's beatings. Once Nikos joined us, the three of us were inseparable and used to go into the woods hunting to get away from pack politics and the shit that went down.

Look at Narah. She'll risk her own life for her sisters. Her devotion is fucking beautiful, all of her is, and her passion for her family has me wanting to do anything to help her.

I glance out from the shadows to Ragnar slipping away from the fringe of woods and onto the river's shore. With my arm around Narah's waist, we slowly move closer through the woods, following him from a distance. If shit gets bad, then I need to be there for Ragnar, but still keep this gorgeous Omega safe.

When we pause in a spot that gives us a good viewpoint, I lower my gaze to Narah. She's looking at me, her amber eyes bright and huge tonight, her hair as dark as the night falls over one shoulder in soft waves. Everything about her is spectacular. The vulnerability washing over her face, her sweet full lips, the way she blinks quickly when she's nervous. It takes all my strength to not claim this Omega for myself.

Her sweet, fruity scent floods every inch of me, and fuck me, but it's exquisite. Even now, all I can think about is scooping her into my arms and pushing her up against a tree, her legs wrapped around my waist, my cock spearing into her, savoring the intense, unyielding arousal that she rises in me.

See, she's every inch the distraction I don't need at this moment, as keeping my thoughts straight grows harder. Especially when I picture kissing her neck, freeing those gorgeous breasts, and making her scream. I want to feel her pussy clenching around my cock, squeezing me as we lose ourselves in carnal pleasure.

Fuck! *Rein it in, man.*

Everything about her weakens me. And as much as Ragnar has made his claim over Narah, he hasn't exactly told us not to. I've always been one to take what I want, and I will make her mine, even when I know she won't be an easy conquest. But I do enjoy a challenge.

Right now, she's frowning and pointing at us, then Ragnar, implying we should go out there to help. I squeeze my hold on her waist a bit more.

"We wait," I mouth the words, to which she huffs.

I shake my head and remind myself I need to keep focused.

The second I got distracted, I missed Ragnar darting out of the woods and toward the enemy. Now, I watch him move low as any predator does, having tapped into his wolf, and strike one of the men from behind with perfect precision. His arm locks around his throat and tears him backward. In a swift move, the loud crack of the dude's neck says everything. The man falls to the ground as the second one attacks Ragnar.

Tension jolts through my body, the eagerness to join him, to help him. That rush of adrenaline pushes me to dart forward, but I grind my jaw and wait.

Not yet.

Jae stumbles back, and Narah calls her, waving and pulling against me to be seen. I step with her out into the open while my focus is locked on the deadly roll of battle between Ragnar and his opponent. I have no idea which of the two pricks is Martell, but I have no doubt Ragnar will end his life swiftly if he hasn't already. And that can't come fast enough. Prick is long overdue for death.

Narah runs to her sister and hugs her, their happy cries have my chest clenching. I had never planned to feel these things for this Omega, but even now, her sweet scent is in my nostrils. All I want is to hold her in my arms, which says a lot, seeing as I love to fight.

I lift my attention to where the enemy slips free from Ragnar, but my Alpha gets up nimbly and catches the man's shoulder with a clawed hand. Ragnar's partially transformed, a trick I notice he likes to use often. The man pivots and Ragnar slams him to the ground then straddles his chest, seizing his throat. The man has no chance of moving this mountain off him.

I stroll toward them, and the sucker looks at me, desperation in his eyes. He's gotta know he's not going to survive this...or does he think because Ragnar hasn't killed him yet, he has a sliver of hope?

"I have only one question for you. Answer it, and you might just save your pathetic ass," Ragnar snarls.

The man's eyes are like disks, his face splattered with his own blood and pale as snow. "O-okay," he slurs.

"Good, we have an understanding then," Ragnar continues. "How the fuck did you find the girl and my men in town?"

The guy is struggling to draw in breath, and his lips are already turning blue. He's hitting Ragnar's forearm.

"You're choking him," I say.

"Am I?" he answers, never taking his eyes off the man, and I notice he softens his grip a bit. "Speak!"

"The witches," he gurgles. "They told Martell where she'd be."

I stiffen at his admission. What the fuck? The witches played us?

"Why?" Ragnar hollers, shaking the man by his neck. The man's spurting blood from his mouth. He's in bad shape.

"S-savage S-sector. T-they promised the sector."

"What the fuck did he just say?" I snap, but Ragnar only growls, his arm holding the guy bulging with veins and muscles from how hard he's choking him. The man's thrashing, desperate for escape, but we lose him fast. His eyes roll back, and he goes limp.

Ragnar releases him and tilts his head up, unleashing a tremendous howl that has zilch to do with calling other wolves. The sound he makes is primal and vicious. He's furious.

Savage Sector is ours... and that snot head Martell thinks he can take it.

Ragnar gets to his feet, wiping his bloody hands on his pants. "Those fucking backstabbing bitches. I'm going to destroy the High Priestess for playing me, then burn down the whole fucking Poisonous Woods."

"But if they knew where Jae was the whole time, why didn't they just take her themselves? These fuckheads who kidnapped her had gone right past the witch's forest."

Blowing out a loud exhale, Ragnar scrubs his face. "Isn't it obvious? It's not Jae the witches want. It's something else. We need to work that out fast and pray we're not wrong." Then he glances up to where Narah and Jae are watching. His expression is dark, but he doesn't say anything to them. They would have heard everything.

"Stay with the girls. I'm going out to check on Crius and Nikos," he orders.

I nod as Ragnar approaches the water's edge and splashes his face and hands before crossing; the water sloshes against him, coming up to his thighs.

"Everything will be okay," I say to both of them.

Narah's snuggling up against her sister, but the heavy burden on Narah's face matches how I feel on the inside. We've walked in on something with the witches, and they've decided to use us. I just don't know if that makes us the bait in their scheme.

"I'm never leaving you behind again," Narah says to her sister with a soft but firm voice, drawing my attention as she wipes tears from Jae's cheeks.

"You better not," Jae answers softly. The young sister has definitely grown on me since our trip collecting her from the Shadowlands Sector. Despite everything she's been through, she always finds a way to make a joke of it, to appear stronger even in the scariest of moments. But seeing her now, crying in Narah's arms, shows how vulnerable this young girl is. And she deserves protection from this cruel world... just as much as Narah.

"It's good to have you back," I say to Jae.

"Took your time, you big lug." She punches me in the arm, but I'm not blind to the paleness of her face, to how much less she's smiling now. She must have been terrified.

"Was Martell even with the guys who took you?" I ask Jae, and I notice Narah is too busy staring at Ragnar getting out of the water to pay attention to us.

"Nope. The weasel sent his men to collect me on his behalf. But the men were saying Martell is furious and wants Narah back." She glances over to her sister, her lips thinning like it hurts her to say it. "He's threatened to raze the world and everyone in it to get her."

My hackles rise. "Like fuck he is!" The moment I meet Martell, I'm going to kill him. It's that simple.

Narah

I feel like someone just sucker-punched me right in the solar plexus, and I can't draw breath. I don't want to overthink why the witches lied to us and why they sold out Jae. Was it to make sure we failed our mission? But to not find my ex was an enormous blow. "Martell needed to be here to die today."

Jae nods and hugs me. "I'm just glad you saved me. Let's not worry about Martell right now."

I hug her back and kiss the top of her head. "Me too, sis."

We have enough problems, so eliminating Martell would have been a blessing. But now he'll send more men, and I shake with anger. But, unlike the first time, I have no plans of whimpering in his presence. I'm going to hurt him with every ounce of magic I have.

The crunch of foliage has us all turning our attention to the bank across the river. Ragnar's slapping the water from his pants while Crius is strolling out from the woods behind him, splattered in blood.

I gasp at the sight, my mouth falling open, expecting him to topple over. But instead, he saunters to the river and washes his bloodied axe like nothing in the world matters.

"See you left nothing for me," Crius says loud enough for us to hear.

"Looks like you've had your fair share of fun," Ragnar answers, already making his way back through the water toward us.

But when a groan comes from behind us, I startle and grab Jae, who gasps as I push her away from the sound.

I turn, half expecting to see an undead.

But instead, it's Nikos stumbling out from the shadows, clutching his gut. Blood running freely from between his fingers. He looks up, meeting my eyes, and beneath the moon's light, I see the terror in his gaze and the paleness of his skin. And it scares the hell out of me.

Suddenly, he drops to his knees.

My stomach churns, and I hurry over to him, a chill enveloping me. "Nikos!"

Footsteps close in behind me, along with the splash of water, telling me Crius and Ragnar are running toward us too.

I reach Nikos and drop next to him, my eyes locked on his hands pressing against his middle, and all the blood. Fear has my heart rattling in my chest.

"I'm fine," he groans.

"Fuck, you look like shit," Crius mutters.

"Geez, state the obvious," Jae responds. I adore her so much.

"Great, now we've got two Narahs giving me attitude," he murmurs, almost jokingly.

"Crius, stop being a dick," I say, my insides twisting with anguish. "Go get the fucking horses. Do something. Nikos is seriously hurt."

He snarls and marches back to where we'd left the horses. Stone is on his heels. I can hear their climbing voices but not words, and in moments, both are sprinting to collect the horses. Whatever Stone told him has got him to stop being an ass.

Ragnar gently gets Nikos to lie on his back. "Let's see how bad it is."

"I-it's just a knife wound," Nikos murmurs. "I killed both bastards."

"You did great," Ragnar says, turning his attention to where Niko is holding his wound.

Nikos' skin is sweaty, and he's trembling. Fear drums through my mind of how terribly injured he is, and we're in the middle of nowhere. What if he bleeds to death?

Ragnar moves Nikos' hand from the wound, and a gush of blood pours out.

It feels like I'm drowning in ice water. "Oh, goddess, that's bad." I regret saying that instantly. I don't want to scare Nikos, but I'm pretty sure he knows it himself.

Ragnar quickly takes off his coat, then yanks the shirt up and over his head, so he's bare-chested. He folds the fabric and places it under Nikos' hand. "You'll need to apply pressure to the wound until we can get you stitched up."

Nikos nods, and I jump to my feet, as does Ragnar. "He may need more than stitches," I say. "I don't even know how close we are to a town."

Jae is kneeling beside Nikos, wiping the perspiration from his brow, telling him he better not die on her. Her words are like spears to my heart, and I blink to stop the tears from falling.

"We're not too far from a nearby village," Ragnar explains, the lines at the edges of his mouth deepening, like they do when he's worried. "We just need to be fast and pray nothing gets in our way."

My breath catches in my throat as cold sweat licks over my skin. I hate feeling like I can never catch a break, and now my bad luck has rubbed off on the guys.

"But he'll pull through," he tells me, yet I hear the quiver beneath his words. "We just need to stop the blood so his wolf can heal him."

I'm not sure who he's trying to convince right now—me or himself.

I nod, needing to believe him, or I'll completely fall apart. I have no choice, and I keep looking back over to where the other two vanished, wishing they'd hurry the heck up.

Pain surges through me that Nikos is in a lot more trouble than anyone wants to admit.

There's just so much blood.

12

NARAH

Overgrown fields surround us. I'm on the back of the horse, clinging to Stone as we rush to get Nikos help. Orange lights glint in the distance like beacons in the darkness—the small village Ragnar promises will aid Nikos.

Of course, I'm skeptical about trusting any other Alphas, and I have Jae to look out for, but what choice do we have? We need to stick together, and if we do nothing, Nikos will die. So, we all push forward, and I pray to the moon goddess.

Please keep us all safe.

Nikos is slumped on his horse, but he's riding next to Ragnar, who holds onto his reins.

Despite the chill setting over the night, Stone's back is like a furnace, and I have no problems at all warming myself against him.

"You okay back there?" he asks, his hand on mine, which are looped around his middle.

"I'm fine. But how does Ragnar know we can trust the Alphas in this pack?"

"They've sworn partial allegiance to him."

I nod even though he can't see me, and knowing Ragnar has some control over the place we're going to fills me with some confidence that we'll be safe. I fall silent after that and listen to the horses galloping like thunder down the road.

I keep staring at the way Nikos sways on his horse and how Ragnar nudges him to not fall unconscious. I keep my head low as we race across the flat land. I don't know how long it's taken us since we left the woods, but we finally slow down, and I lift my gaze as we turn down a path flanked by pines.

We approach a lofty iron gate, with a chain-link fence jutting out in either direction, encasing the pack's territory.

Ragnar has jumped off his horse and is talking to a guard who carries a shotgun. I can't tell if that's for the undead or other wolves...my guess is the latter. Numerous packs have claimed small pockets of land in Savage Sector, but there is no overarching Alpha, so it's each wolf or pack for himself out here.

In moments, the gates open with a metallic groan, and I breathe easier at the lack of trouble. Ragnar climbs back up on his horse, then we are off again.

I glance at the guard as we pass him, and see he's watching us, mostly Jae and me. Does he think we're commodities brought in to offer for sale? How wrong he is, as I'd never let that happen to my sisters or me. I lift my chin as he turns to shut the gate behind us.

We come to a stop in front of a set of stone steps that look worn from weather, pavers cracked and grass growing between them. Two sets of fiery torches flank the entrance and on either side is an explosion of shrubs that look semi-trimmed like someone really tried to make them look manicured.

We all get off our horses as three men emerge from the darkness behind us. For all I know, there could be stables just around the corner, but I honestly can't see them in the dark.

Crius talks to them about a place for our horses to feed and rest, and there's no argument.

Everything's happening so fast my head spins. Jae clings to me, shaking. She's been through so much already; she deserves to feel safe.

Ragnar and Stone have Nikos between them, their arms around his back, and they carry him up the stairs.

I take Jae's hand and pull her in the same direction. "Let's stay close to them."

We're on their heels, my attention alert. At the top of the steps, enormous flat land stretches outward, surrounded by more woodland. The place looks like it might have once been one of those human parks I've read about in books. Except in this space, there are maybe fifty or more wooden cabins with pointy roofs around the perimeter in several lines, and in the middle is a roaring bonfire, spitting embers into the sky.

The guys move swiftly to the second cabin on the right, knowing exactly where they're going. The ground is mostly dirt and pebbles, and to the side of the home, I spot a vegetable garden. It reminds me of being back with the Storm Wolves. My gut twists, remembering a time when I thought we were safe and how that turned out. Might explain why I'm constantly looking over my shoulder, and my skin pricks at every sound.

Crius gives a loud bang on the arched door, and it is opened in seconds by an older man with white hair. He's dressed in brown leather pants and a matching vest with no shirt underneath. And his skin is deeply tanned. His eyes widen immediately as if he's shocked but also pleased with our interruption in the middle of the night. Then he notices Nikos.

"Ragnar, come in quickly." He waves us to enter, and I pull Jae alongside me, both of us glued side-by-side.

"Mihai, it's great to see you again."

Before stepping inside, I notice people emerging from nearby homes to check on the commotion, no doubt, but I duck my head low and enter.

The cabin is surprisingly large. Blankets and cushions for seating steal half the space, which tells me a big family could live here. Along the back wall, there's a fire oven and a table with six chairs, and at the rear is a hallway, which I assume leads to more rooms.

"Place him here." The man shoves aside the cushions to make a clearing for Nikos on the blanket, and the men set him down. I hurry over to them and tuck a pillow under his head.

He's clutching his side, groaning, and my blood runs cold. He's always been this powerful Alpha, so to see him this way is painful. I've lost enough people and have witnessed so much death that my chest constricts at his suffering.

Blood drenches his shirt and hands. It drips over his fingers, and my heart is in my throat. Jae's next to me, clutching me tightly.

"We'll be alright," I whisper to her. She's watching everyone, not taking her eyes off the old man.

"I apologize for our abrupt arrival in the middle of the night. But you were the closest place and friend to call upon for help." Ragnar stands to face the man.

"Ragnar, you can call my pack home." He slaps a hand to his shoulder, then turns his head and hollers, "Lyssa, girl, get out here now. Ragnar has come to visit." Then he faces Ragnar with a wide grin. "Your friend will need stitching by the looks of it." He goes into the kitchen and collects a bucket from a pantry along with a bottle of what I guess is alcohol.

I look down at Nikos. His face is tight, eyes scrunched up. When he opens them, he tries to smile, but it comes out lopsided and painful.

"N-Narah," he begins, but I shake my head.

"You don't need to talk. Just hold on. Someone's going to fix you." My throat closes up, and my eyes prick with tears. I've held it together this long, so I'm not going to lose it now. Jae rubs my back. She's always been good at sensing my emotions, and I should be celebrating that I have her, but instead, I'm worried sick about Nikos.

Crius, who's kneeling across from me, has his hands on the wound, applying pressure. Nikos looks as pale as a ghost. He lost so much blood during the ride here.

"You better not die on me," I whisper to Nikos. "I just started to really like you."

I sense Crius watching me, listening, but I can't hide away in private with Nikos to tell him he has no right to die.

Crius reaches over with his other hand and slides loose hair off my face. "He's going to survive. He's a fucking tough bastard, and he's not going anywhere."

I want Nikos to tell me the same thing, but when I meet his gaze, his eyes are fluttering like he's going to pass out.

"Hold on," I tell him. "Please, Nikos."

Footsteps striking the wooden floorboards have me glancing up to a woman, maybe eighteen or nineteen years old, with flowing blonde hair that tumbles over her shoulders and to her waist. She's frantically tying a blue robe around herself, her eyes blinking away sleep. Her gaze sweeps over the strangers in her home.

"Ragnar," she says softly, like he's the only person in the room she actually notices, and takes quick steps to his side, sticking her chest out.

What the heck?

"It has been too long since you've come to visit. I was starting to get worried you've forgotten me."

"Lyssa," the old man growls. "I'm sure you and Ragnar can get reacquainted later, but for now, there is a man dying on the floor."

Lyssa huffs, and her smile drops. She turns to the man, frowning. "Did you get the alcohol, Father?" Her tone is almost scolding.

"Everything is waiting for you," he replays with a harsh voice and points to Nikos' feet where he'd laid the bucket, bandages, and everything else she needs.

The silence in the room is deafening.

She purses her lips, raises her head, and walks toward us, her eyes on Nikos. "I need space," she snaps, cutting me a sharp look.

Okay, someone has a chip on her shoulder. "I'm staying with Nikos," I answer adamantly. "And I can help you."

"Wonderful idea," her father answers. "Ragnar, let's talk in the kitchen."

Lyssa's hazel eyes narrow in disbelief, but she doesn't respond. Instead, she kneels next to Nikos and pulls back Crius' hand and fabric to inspect the injury.

"Ouch, this looks deep." She scrunches up her nose.

"Are you a healer?" Jae asks while my fingers flip open the buttons on Nikos' shirt, and my thoughts fly to us together, how the slightest touch left me breathless, and how he showed me euphoria so easily that even now, my body tingles. I don't want to lose the chance to do that again, to fall asleep in his arms. So, I pull the shirt down his shoulders, and Jae helps me slide it off him.

"Something like that," Lyssa answers Jae despondently.

Nikos whimpers, and I place a hand on his arm, so he knows I'm there for him. "You're going to be okay," I reassure him, though I have no idea if he can even make sense of what I'm saying.

Ragnar and Stone move to the rear of the room, and the old man serves them a clear drink from a long-necked bottle at the table. Crius sniffs the air and is on his feet in an instant, making his way to others. "Be back in a sec," he says.

"My name's Narah," I say to Lyssa. "And this is my sister, Jae."

"Why are you with Ragnar and his pack? Is he selling you two to Alphas in town?" She doesn't look at me as she speaks, but is dabbing the blood from the injury with a folded-up towel.

Nikos groans, and I squeeze his shoulder slightly.

"We're not for sale," I respond instantly as Jae moves to Nikos' other side and wipes the perspiration from his face. "They're helping me."

Her head juts up, and her eyes flash on me, then over to Ragnar at the table. "What sort of help?"

I shrug. "It doesn't really matter." Telling her anything sounds like a terrible idea, considering my initial impression of this girl. My instincts scream not to trust her and that she seems to have some crazy obsession withRagnar.

Not that I can blame her. The guy is a god and built like one too. After our time in the Poisonous Woods, the witches, them protecting me, and the mark he gave me, one can say each of these men has grown on me. More than I should have allowed, but nothing in my life is predictable now, is it?

But as I watch Lyssa cleaning Nikos' wound and how she keeps sneaking a look over to the men by the table, I'm wondering what exactly her story with Ragnar is. She's extremely beautiful with her porcelain skin, large eyes, heart-shaped lips, and has curves in all the right places. The girl is stunning; I doubt any man could say no to her.

The longer I study her, the more self-doubt hits me. I can't compete with her. I'm nowhere as pretty as her, not with that bone structure, and her breasts made to be noticed. I want to cover myself up in her presence, as I must look like a mess.

It's clear she and Ragnar have a history, and I hate that it stirs a lick of jealousy through me.

"Put your hand here and press down," she says, tearing me from my thoughts. "Make yourself useful. Splash his injury with this." She shoves the bottle of alcohol into my other hand. It smells of over-ripe plums, and it feels like my nostrils are burning from breathing it in. I squint my eyes at how damn strong this is.

Lyssa starts threading a needle, getting ready to stitch up Nikos. The thing with wolves is that they should mostly heal themselves from any injury, as long as it's not a mortal blow, but that means stopping his blood loss.

I press my hand down on the folded towel to apply pressure and lift the bottle to get ready to disinfect his wound.

"Want me to pour," Jae offers.

"No, it's okay. I'll do it," I answer, not wanting her to even see this, but I guess she's already witnessed so many horrific things in this world, even at just fourteen years of age.

"Nikos, this is going to sting a bit. I'm sorry."

He nods, his jaw clenching. Jae hands him a pillow. "Here, squeeze this."

Lyssa is sniggering.

I look at her, annoyed by her rudeness. "What's so funny?"

"You two are doting over this Alpha. Have you two been living under a rock most of your lives? Alphas don't give a shit about us Omegas, so you don't need to pretend in front of me. No matter how hot they are, don't become their slaves. Learn to play the game and always look out for number one. Yourself." She smirks and glances at Nikos, who is too out of it to really pay attention to what she's saying. "So while this guy is too hurt to stop us, who says we can't make him suffer a bit longer, if you get my drift," she whispers so no one else can hear her.

The funny thing is that before I met Ragnar and his men, I would have been exactly the same way, taking any chance to stab an Alpha in the back. And most deserve so much worse, but I struggle to accept that for Nikos.

I'd just been close to crying over him, and now this crazy girl is telling me to torture him.

"While I'd normally agree with you, in this case, just no. I want him out of pain," I state. "I won't let you hurt him more than he already is."

She shrugs. "Whatever."

I shake my head, my heart hammering in my chest that I'd just stuck up for Nikos... just as he'd fought for me when those other Alphas attacked me near the tavern. Surprisingly, it feels amazing.

Would I hurt Nikos? Could I?

Goddess no!

Absolutely, no.

"You two are the ones who'll regret it later," Lyssa snorts.

But Nikos is watching me, shaking terribly, so I ignore her.

"Okay, hold on to the pillow." Jae pushes it into his hands on his chest, and I peel away the towel, revealing the deep cut where the blade went right into him.

Not wasting time, I grip the neck of the bottle and start splashing the clear liquid over the injury. I'd seen Father do this when he'd caught his leg on barbed wire once. He poured a small amount, then quickly stitched it to stop the bleeding.

Nikos hisses, his body convulsing. A growl rolls from his chest. Jae's forcing the pillow into his hands frantically. "Hold on to this," she keeps telling him over and over.

"Hurry, stitch him," I say to Lyssa, my voice climbing more than it should.

But she's taking her time, fiddling with the blue thread. I'm going to grab that needle and do it myself if she doesn't hurry the hell up.

"You can't trust them." She leans in closer, and I shuffle aside, but instead of working faster, she whispers to me, "I mean, Ragnar has promised to wed me, but that doesn't mean he'll treat me fair or that I'll be the most trusting wife." She winks at me, grinning.

I shudder at her words, breathing so hard that stars dance in my vision. Jae is saying something, but I can't hear her over the hammering of my heart. "You're marrying him?" I gasp, when Nikos suddenly bellows.

I look around to find that I'm spilling more of the booze onto his wound and splashing it everywhere.

"Watch it," Jae cries, snatching more cushions from around her to pat Nikos dry.

I set the bottle down away from us, and Lyssa sews his wound. The rest of the men are looking our way, so she finally gets to work.

I shuffle closer to Nikos and hold his hand. Darkness shrouds his gaze, and he's grinding his teeth through the pain. I wince for him, feeling awful for causing him more pain. All I can do while Lyssa sews him up is stare at him writhing on the floor.

Everything about him is rugged and beautiful, from the sharpness of his cheekbones to his chiseled jawline and even those kissable lips. Being next to him ignites something within me. I can't lose him. My hand runs over his brow, wiping the perspiration away.

His chest raises up and down with each rapid breath he takes as he rides the wave of pain, the muscles in his neck corded and tense.

With a snip of the string with her teeth, Lyssa finishes stitching the wound. She grabs the bandages, mainly strips of fabric, and folds one in half several times before pressing it over the stitches. She wraps the longer pieces around his middle. Jae and I help with getting the material under him and back around for Lyssa to tie so it stays in place.

"Done." She gets to her feet and wipes her hands, then takes the bucket of bloody water into the hallway, vanishing.

"Do you think he'll be okay?" Jae asks. I stare down at Nikos, whose eyes are closed and breathing grows heavy, seeming to have passed out to allow his body to heal.

"Of course," I respond with my best confident voice, even if on the inside, I'm asking the same question as my sister. I want to be strong for her, to take the agony from her if I can, even if it feels like my heart is being strangled every time I look at Nikos.

"By the way." She leans over to me, muttering, "I don't trust Lyssa."

"That makes two of us. We need to be careful while we're in this village."

Everything has an alcoholic stench, and I reach for Nikos' shirt, which needs washing.

"I've just saved your friend," Lyssa sing-songs loudly as she waltzes back into the room, drawing everyone's attention. She saunters right toward Ragnar, standing so close to him, she's practically rubbing her breasts on his arm.

I stare, the sight like torture, while a fire burns over my heart.

Jae collects the rest of the bandages Lyssa forgot and goes up to her, interrupting her flirting with Ragnar to hand them to her. Crius makes his way back over to me and takes my hand, pulling up to my feet.

He's close to me, barely an inch between us, and my knees wobble. "I saw the way you were looking at Lyssa," he says quietly. "I don't want you to even let yourself think such things. You are a goddess in my eyes, in all our eyes. She is nothing to us."

"Crius," the old man calls to him, and with a quick smile my way, he returns to the table.

If that's true, why did Lyssa say Ragnar was marrying her?

13

RAGNAR

Narah moans, struggling to wake up. I sit by her bed, watching her. She's so beautiful. I'm tempted to crawl under the blankets and fuck her. To take her over and over, to remind her that she is mine.

She stirs and suddenly opens her eyes, staring at me, almost startled. She pushes out from under the blankets with speed. That's when she looks around and gasps, "Where's Jae? Is Nikos okay?"

"They're fine, little fox. In fact, Jae's with the kitchen girls preparing tonight's meal, as she insisted on helping. Something about learning how to cook something other than fire-roasted rabbit. And Nikos is awake, healing. He'll need another day or so."

Softness sweeps over Narah's face, and she collapses back on the edge of the bed. "Is it sad that my first reaction was to expect imminent danger?" She's got her hand over her chest. "My heart is beating so fast right now."

I can't even laugh because I understand that all too well. "If it makes you feel better, I woke up sweating, thinking we were back in the Poisonous Woods." Not to mention I woke up yelling thirteen days. The exact number of days we have left before the curse strangles us. This shit is getting to me.

She laughs. "That place still gives me nightmares, too." I glance at her nightdress that falls to her knees. It's white and made of extremely thin fabric. It takes everything I have to hold her stare and not devour those rosy nipples standing tight behind the material. My intention had never been to claim her when I struck a deal with her initially. I have my own shit to do, but since catching up with her in town after finding Jae, I lost part of myself to this girl.

It seems I stopped fighting my inner demons about letting another woman into my life after my fated mate rejected me, but Narah is different from my ex. She is similar to me. We have darkness in our pasts, and it feels like we're on the same side.

"Come here." I take her hand, guiding her to stand between my legs, and my fingers slide to her waist. She's so soft and small next to me. "How are you feeling?"

"Like I could sleep the entire day." She gives me a wonky smile and yawns.

"Sorry to tell you, but you've already done that."

She tilts her head toward the window behind me, and her cute mouth drops open with shock. She's just too gorgeous. When she looks back at me, I kiss her, needing to taste her sweetness, to hear her moans, to have her breasts against me. If I could, I'd press her into me so nothing could touch her again.

Narah's been through hell, which has made her stronger. I see the fire in her eyes, in her actions, so hiding her away won't work. She's a fighter, so I'll take my spot by her side as her warrior and defend her. I may not know what will happen tomorrow, but I am adamant that I'll make her mine... even if she doesn't know it yet.

She's kissing me back without hesitation, then suddenly stiffens and breaks away.

"What's wrong?" It worries me to see her smile fade.

Untangling herself from my hold, she stumbles backward and sits back on the bed. "I need to know something first," she says, her words shaky, and she's holding her hands in her lap.

"Of course. Anything."

"It's just that my fated mate, Martell, broke parts of me when he rejected our bond. He broke the wings I thought I had to soar with in this world, but his actions brought out my claws. Before I found you, I thought I lost everything and I was at the lowest point in my life. I don't ever want to feel like that again because I trusted the wrong man."

I ease forward to the edge of my seat. "Little fox, what are you talking about?" I get to my feet, my chest tightening, and I sit by her side on the bed.

"I just want you to be honest with me because Lyssa told me you were going to marry her. Maybe it's just her daydreaming that she will be with you because, I mean, look at you. But I need to be sure."

She's doing that thing where she rambles when she's nervous, and it's cute, but her words are like a thorn in my side. Of course, Lyssa would have told her at the first chance she got, and I should have prepared her for it beforehand. But everything happened so fast.

"It's not that simple," I answer.

She's on her feet and turning to face me. "It's actually a pretty simple question. You are or aren't planning to marry her?" She assesses me, watching me for my reaction, but I don't feel guilty when I have nothing to feel guilty about.

But seeing her worked up does bug me.

I get up and walk to her. She recoils from me. "She is nothing to me. Never was and never will be. She doesn't hold a candle to you, little fox, so you have nothing to be jealous about."

She rears back and pulls from me. "You haven't answered my question. And this has nothing to do with jealousy. But maybe the fault is mine. For some reason, I thought you said you cared for me, and I foolishly believed it."

Fuck.

"Narah." I march after her and grab her by the arms before pinning her against the wall, caging her with my body.

She slams her hands to my chest. "Get off me."

"Not until you listen to me. Lyssa is nothing to me. She is the Alpha's daughter, and when I first arrived in Romania, they were the first pack I encountered. I made a deal with them to gain a foothold in Savage

Sector, and the only way the Alpha agreed was if I said I'd take his daughter as mine. I had no choice and said yes, but told him it wouldn't happen until I conquered all of Savage Sector."

Her eyes widen, and her chin trembles. Fucking hell. It kills me to see the ache in her eyes.

"I had no intention of doing so. I am biding my time until I gain enough traction that I will overpower his pack." I reach over and place a hand to the side of her face, but she draws from me. A blade might as well be piercing through my chest.

My mother used to say that pain changes people, making them trust less, assuming everyone is out to harm them. But I never wanted Narah to feel that way toward me.

"Say something, gorgeous," I demand.

"I don't know." She blinks, looking away from me, and that stings. "She seemed adamant you were hers."

"I never want to hurt you, but I never said I wasn't a bastard to others. I will do what I need to win over this sector, but one thing I won't compromise on is you. I have nothing to hide from you."

"And what if I was in your shoes? What would you do?" She lifts her head, holding my gaze bravely.

"I'd kill the man," I growl, jealousy erupting through me at the thought. "I can be a jealous Alpha and, little fox, when I marked you in the woods with my bite, I staked my claim. There is no going back for me... I need you to understand this. No one will come between us, no fucking girl, no ex-fated mates."

Her chin trembles. "A-Any man?"

I'm holding onto her shoulders now, and her small hands are on mine, slightly shaking. Does she doubt that I'd kill someone who tries to take her from me?

"As far as I'm concerned," I continue. "From the moment I fucked you, there was no question about what I wanted. You are mine. And I'll do anything for you."

She has this look of innocence that drives me crazy, that tells me she is full of all the best kinds of good and bad. "You may very well be my undoing if you don't destroy me first," I murmur.

"I-I never expected any of this," she says softly. "My feelings are confusing, my past haunts me, and all I ask is for you to be gentle with me. I keep telling myself I shouldn't be drawn to you, but when you say things like that, I stand no chance. But I don't want to be hurt again, Ragnar." The way she looks at me, smiling, gives me the impression she's barely holding back her tears.

Agony spears through my chest, and my lungs are pumping furiously for each breath. "Narah, under different circumstances, I would have told you about Lyssa before we arrived here."

She nods, and I lean in closer to her, stealing a kiss, needing to have her against me to stop the ache pulsing under my breastbone. Her body melts against mine. When we're together, the world falls away and all that remains is us. The desperation to bite her, to make sure the mark sticks harder this time, pulses in my veins.

I want to fuck her again.

My racing heart bangs louder, and my broken thoughts tell me I can't lose her. I'm still reeling from losing my head and heart so fast, but I can't fully take the blame. The growl in my chest has my wolf just as much responsible. He connected with her wolf both times I took her.

A loud knock comes at the door.

"Fuck off," I bark back.

"Ragnar, the pack Alpha, Mihai, is waiting for you to join their meal. Actually, everyone's waiting," Stone states.

"Goddammit." I swallow hard and look at my Narah, desperate to remain with her, convince her she's mine and that no other woman will do. But that's not going to happen. "I have to go," I whisper to her, our brows touching.

"What's going on?"

"When an Alpha invites me for a meal while I'm in his home, it would be an insult to not attend. So, I'll go and play the games." Frustration simmers beneath my skin at having to leave her.

"That's fine," she says and ducks her head under my arm, then crosses the room before opening the door to Stone. "He's all yours."

Something in my gut tells me we weren't finished with the conversation. "We'll talk later." Then I head outside and turn to Stone. "Stay close and watch both her and Jae."

"You got it," he says, and I walk away. With Nikos still injured and Crius out on a hunting mission with the locals to help bring in game for the villagers, a request we couldn't say no to, I guess I'm doing the honorary guest dinner alone.

But all I want is to be buried deep in Narah and convince her I want no one else.

"Can you believe you'll be running this pack in the future?" Lyssa whispers in my ear, leaning so close I'm suffocating from her bitter scent.

Her father, Mihai, watches from the end of the long table, his grin wide. The banquet before us is made of large roasts, a variety of baked bread, and hearty stews. Crius will be pissed he missed this dinner, but he'll eat plenty when he returns, and Stone will ensure Nikos, Narah, and Jae all get a good meal. My mouth salivates at the smells, and the dozen pack members around us greedily dig into the food like such an offering is not a frequent event.

I don't remember some of their names, but I don't care. The way I see it, I will take over this pack and rule soon enough, but not the way they envisage. With Narah as my queen by my side, not Lyssa. I am adamant about this... even if Narah needs convincing that she is the only one for me.

"I will, of course, be by your side," Lyssa continues and strokes my thigh. Her touch is grating on my nerves. It's funny how meeting someone who connects with me, with my wolf, changes my perception. On my first arrival to this pack, I had no problems flirting with

Lyssa. She is a beautiful woman, but now her touch repels me.

Does Narah even realize what she's done to me?

Mihai raises a cup of wine that sloshes over the rim and splashes the table. "A toast to a most auspicious night, having Ragnar Ulv join us. To the union, we will gain between our packs, and my support, which I pledge to aid you in gaining control of the Savage Sector."

I take my cup as the men around us cheer and jut their drinks into the air before guzzling them down. I follow suit to show my respect, then stand for no reason other than to remove Lyssa's hand from my groin.

"You are the first pack to welcome me into your home, and that will be something I won't forget. Our unity will be of tremendous benefit to us all." I raise my drink, figuring maybe being forced to come to this pack right now might be opportune after all. Father had a saying that's always stuck with me: Keep your allegiances strong, even if it means visiting them for a drink once a full moon. The glint in Mihai's eyes reassures me he'll have my back when the time comes. And while I won't take his daughter as mine, I will rule his pack.

"Here's to reigning over the Savage Sector!" I unleash a howl, the sound echoing in the long meal hall.

Everyone jumps to their feet, their heads tilt back, and they join my song of success. Even Lyssa, whom, I have no doubt, will easily find an Alpha to take her.

We fall back into chatter and eating when Lyssa presses into my shoulder.

"Hearing you speak like that gave me goosebumps, all the way down between my thighs," she whispers in my ear. "I give you permission to touch and find out."

I swallow the mouthful of venison I just took a bite of and twist toward her. Her blond hair is swept off her face tonight and plaited. Small white flowers adorn her hair, akin to a halo. Her pale eyes never leave mine, and her crimson lips pull into a grin.

My earlier words come back to me. The ones my dad had made about keeping appearances with those you make pacts with, and last time I'd visited, Lyssa shared a secret with me.

"I'd like to ask a favor of you," I murmur.

Her eyes grow in size, and she shuffles closer to me, which I didn't think was possible.

"Of course. Ask me anything." She places a hand on my leg, and as much as I'd like to push away her advances, I may need to play the part a while longer.

"My friend needs your assistance. She's looking for her mother, and you spoke highly of your seer abilities on my last visit."

Her spine stiffens at my words, and she studies me carefully. "If you don't mind me asking, who are those two Omegas? Are you selling them?" There is a flick of jealousy in her eyes, and to tell her the truth would not aid our cause.

"They're family friends." Reluctantly, I reach over and cup her face, my fingers tenderly holding her, my thumb sweeping over her cheek.

She softens against my touch, but I feel nothing at this moment. No attraction, no arousal, no wolf shoving forward, as he had in Narah's presence.

"Will you do this for me?"

She has eyes only for me like there is no one else in the room with us. And I can see many men falling for the beauty in her eyes, but not me.

"Only for you, I'll help."

She leans in quickly and kisses my cheek, then whispers, "Maybe tonight you should visit my room. I'll leave the window open."

I hate leading her on, but when a hand claps roughly on my shoulder, I gratefully pull from Lyssa and turn to find her father behind me.

"Ragnar, come and warm yourself by the fire with me. Let's talk," he announces.

"Of course." I'm on my feet instantly, more than thankful to leave the table, and follow him across the room to the roaring fireplace.

"You've arrived at a good time, as I have given our union much thought." He stares into the fire, his pause telling me this isn't a general discussion about taking over the sector. He wants something more from me.

"You have agreed to take my daughter, and in exchange, my pack is at your disposal to use for expanding your territory. We've already taken over three packs in the nearby lands, and we have four more in sight. But I feel that my leg work and responsibility greatly outweighs yours."

I bristle at his implication, but I swallow back my pride. "I am always on your side, Mihai, so tell me how I can correct this? And don't forget, I have my own pack of at least fifty men too, and my deal with the witches, which will give us an advantage over everyone." I grind my teeth, needing to stretch the truth somewhat. He doesn't need to know the current circumstances with the witches.

"My men are starved of women. For a pack of two hundred men, we have ten Omegas, so you can imagine the trouble this causes. The lands are so sparse of females, and I fear I'll soon have a mutiny on my hands as the men leave to find a mate to claim."

Distant voices and laughter from the table fill the void while my thoughts come to one quick solution. Ever since the virus ravaged our world and killed most of the people, females have become fewer in number and so rarely found.

But on my recent trip to the Shadowlands Sector, I discovered a larger number of females live in the south of the country.

Dušan is the Alpha of the Shadowlands Sector and, on our last encounter, I'd told him I would pay him another visit, seeing as he was having some issues of his own. Seems someone close to him had tried to take over the pack... either way, it doesn't bother me how that turned out. I made him a promise.

"What promise I will make is that I will return to your land with my warriors. If you are not in charge upon my arrival,

and this mess hasn't been swept away, I will wipe out all the males on this land, claim the females, and take ownership."

Dušan stands tall and proud. He doesn't get defensive, and already I can tell he's an Alpha I respect. He finally answers, "If I do not reclaim my sector by the next blue moon, I will not stand in your way. But when we do meet again, I propose we make arrangements for our packs to work together."

I glance up at Mihai, who's watching me, expecting a response. I clear my throat, saying, "There's someone I know who can assist. I can get you what you need. Would that alleviate your concerns?"

"At least a hundred Omegas," he demands.

I hold back the urge to scoff at him. He's fucking kidding. "Twenty, and we have a deal," I growl my response. My shoulder blades bunch up now that I need to somehow add a trip to the south with my list of growing problems.

"Sixty," he counters.

"Forty, and that's my final offer. I will bring them to you in a few months."

His brow pinches at my suggestion. "No, my son. You will deliver them within a month if you want to unite with my pack. Otherwise, our agreement is off, and all the packs I'm currently amassing under my reign will end up your enemy."

My wolf's rolling in my chest, teeth bared at this traitor. But I'd do the same in his position… after all, we're all playing to survive.

"Do we have a deal then?" he continues, putting his hand out to shake.

The noose hanging over my head with the witches' curse grows tighter. It's a risk I have to take. Lyssa will hopefully give us directions to Narah's mother, and I pray to the moon goddess that she will be our answer to eradicate the curse with those witches. Maybe even the ability to take them over. We have less than two weeks for that, giving me two more weeks, if I survive, to pay Shadowlands Sector a visit.

Fuck!

I growl under my breath, but know there's no other way around this. I need Mihai and his growing pack, as they will all be under me to help gain more packs under one umbrella. And that means making sacrifices now.

I shake his hand. "Deal."

14

STONE

I shut the door to the bedroom, where Jae is fast asleep. She's exhausted herself after helping in the kitchen, but I haven't seen her smile that much since I met her. The poor thing is dying for some kind of normalcy. I'd gone to find Narah, but she's not here. The small cabin they've given us for our stay means we don't all get a bed. Crius crashed on the blankets near the window, snoring like a dragon after his day of hunting.

Nikos is across the room from him, also snoozing, though he's twitching like he's having a nightmare. On the bright side, he's healing. Soon we can get the hell out of this town and go find Narah's mother. Somehow. I pin my hopes on Ragnar sucking up to the Alpha's daughter and seeing if she can aid us with her seer power. The girl's lost her shit over him and is so smitten, it's kinda sad. Glad it's him and not me having to let her down.

If it wasn't for Narah, Ragnar wouldn't hesitate to take one for the team and sleep with Lyssa to get her to do our bidding, so I am curious to find out how he pulls this off. We've all witnessed how he looks at Narah, and the thing about my Alpha is that he's fucking loyal to those he considers family.

I kick Crius' boots. He crashed fully dressed.

He groans until I kick him again.

"What the fuck, man?" he snarls, opening just one eye.

"Where's Narah?"

He rolls onto his back and opens the other eye. "She said something about going to wash her clothes or something. Now fuck off." He turns away from me and is snoring again in seconds.

I head outside into the cool night, my attention caught by two men near the blazing fire in the middle of all the homes. It makes me wonder if it's something they keep running all the time or not, as that would take a lot of effort.

Reaching the men, I step into their line of sight. "Evening," I say, with some semblance of respect, instead of just demanding they answer my question right away. Hey, I'm trying.

They lift their chin in my direction, not bothering to even respond. Well, so much for that respectful shit.

"Where's the washroom?" I go for something simple, figuring they might understand it easier. They don't seem like the brightest bastards in the shed.

"It's the cabin farthest to your left, right next to the baths," one man grunts, then turns his back to me to keep talking to his friend, who looks my way. "You're after the black-haired beauty with the fuckable ass?" He grins, revealing a missing front tooth. "She looks easy."

His friend chortles, and fuck, these two are pissing me off. They could only be talking about Narah.

A possessiveness rises within me and claws at my chest. I struggle to not shove him into the fire for speaking about her that way, though I am half tempted... except that might ruin our diplomatic standing with this pack. Some days I wish I was more like Crius, who'd have both men already burning.

Instead, I do it my way. I lash out and snatch the man by the throat, then haul him toward me. His friend comes at me, but I punch him square in the nose with my other hand, which has him reeling, backing into the fire. He squeals. Idiot.

I turn to the asshole in front of me, who's growling. He throws a jab into my gut, but I feel nothing when I'm rolling in rage. "You don't get to look at her ever again, speak about her, breathe near her, nothing. Understand? To you, she doesn't exist because she's already claimed. You cross me, and I will rip your fucking heart right out of your chest out next time I see you."

"You son of a—"

I headbutt him even though my runes burn across my chest, my wolf raging through me to rip open the ground, so he falls into the pits of Hell itself. Instead, I shove him out of my face before I give in to my power. He's crying and grasping his bloody nose.

"Fucking pussies," I call after them as they retreat, rubbing the soreness on my forehead from where I struck that asshole. But it's worth it to remind those two of their place.

When I find the washroom empty, I pop my head into the baths just to be sure because if I don't find her, I'm tearing down every damn cabin until I track her down.

Except, once inside, I can't believe my eyes. The gorgeous girl I've been searching for is standing naked with her back to me, sticking her hand into the water of the round wooden tub she's clearly about to climb into. The tub reaches her thighs in height, and she's bending over enough that my cock hardens in a second flat.

My eyes are locked on the sight of her firm, round ass, long legs, slender waist, and—fuck me—but I need her to turn around before I go insane. But I'm not fooling myself. Since spending time with her on our trip into the Poisonous Woods, she's messed me up big time right inside my chest. Could be that I haven't found anyone serious or my fated mate yet. Or that I'm completely blinded by her beauty, her fiery nature, or that she's a survivor like the rest of us.

But who the fuck cares right now. That's not what I want to think about when she's naked. I'm wearing too many clothes. My cock hurts at how hard it is. I need her. All of her.

There's no one else in the room, and as she climbs into the tub, I shut the door behind me. The bang echoes a bit too loud. Narah yelps and falls into the bath, sending a cascade of water sloshing out over the edge. She goes under, then comes gasping back up, her hair slicked back, and stares at me with those doe-eyes, startled.

My attention locks on those perky tits of hers that bounce from her sudden movement, not covered by water, and she completely undoes me.

"What the hell, Stone!" She quickly covers herself and dips lower, so only her head sticks out.

"No use hiding, sweetheart. Already saw everything, and it's fucking delicious."

"Ha, you did not. Wait, are you spying on me?" Her cheeks are beautifully red and damn but I love seeing her this way. The way she gasps, her eyes dilated, the veins in her neck pulsing.

I stroll toward her, unbuttoning my shirt.

"Hmm, what are you doing?" she gasps.

"What does it look like? I'm going to take a bath."

Her gaze narrows on me. "Well this tub isn't big enough for two." She glances at the other two tubs and points to one across the room in a corner. "Go to that one. Looks big enough to fit you, but first, you need to go request hot water."

"Oh, don't you worry, sweetheart. I'll fit." I smirk as I slide the shirt off and drop it to the floor behind me while I pause and toe off my boots.

"I'm serious, Stone. Don't you dare come in here, or I'll drown you."

I burst out laughing, and the urge to fight this vixen while we're both naked has my cock twitching with an unbearable need to finally take what I've been wanting since I first saw her.

I've been meaning to tell this beauty that I intend to claim her as mine. After all, the four of us share everything, and that includes Omegas. Especially Omegas.

And tonight, I have every intention of treating her as my queen, lifting her into the heavens until she looks at me like I'm all she's ever desired. Maybe later, I'll treat her to a foot massage while I feed her grapes with my mouth.

She's still covering her breasts, and liquid fire shoots through my veins.

I unbuckle my pants and drop them. I always go commando.

Her gaze lowers, and her mouth might have just opened into an O shape.

"You like this, don't you? Of course, you do."

She swallows loudly, and no longer tells me to leave.

The thing about Narah is that I've seen the way she looks at me, how her breaths catch, how her scent changes to one of arousal in my presence. No matter what she might say, on the inside, she knows the truth. She wants everything from me, and I intend to give it.

I climb into the tub with her—it is round and can easily fit three people. It's how they're designed—but Narah's at one end, still hiding those gorgeous breasts from me.

"Don't fight this," I say. "Sometimes, following your instincts is not such a bad idea."

I dunk down into the warm embrace and splash myself with water, along with my face and, run wet fingers through my hair. It feels amazing.

"You lost for words?" I ask.

"Just curious why you think you can just get into the bath with me, and it be okay?"

My eyes drag across her body under the water, to where she has her legs bent, and back to her chest. "Because I needed a wash, and you looked inviting."

She snorts a laugh, yet her chest is heaving and, despite her words, she studies my body too.

"Do you like what you see?" she asks.

"Of course I do. You can't tell? But how about we stop talking about this and let me show you that you are mine and what that means."

She smiles sweetly at me, and sometimes it's hard to tell with Narah what she's really up to. "Is that so?" She lowers her knees in the bathtub, revealing her gorgeous breasts and pink nipples.

Reaching down, I grab my dick and squeeze it, imagining it's her tight pussy. I moan under my breath, then move through the water toward her, both of us at eye level.

I love the panicked look in her gaze; it skyrockets my adrenaline.

When I pause in front of her, she grins, then in a sudden movement, she tosses water right in my face. I blink through the cascade, only to find her twisting around and rushing to climb out of the water, that gorgeous ass bending over.

So what's a man to do? I lunge after her, grabbing her hips, and I shove my face into her ass. Resisting is futile, so I give her what she craves. Me.

My tongue laps out and strokes between her cheeks, taking her hungrily. My fingers dig into her sides, and I lick her, dipping lower, needing to taste her juices, her sweet scent already engulfing every inch of me.

She moans. I love the way she responds to my touch. Instead of pushing me away, she holds onto the padding that winds around the top of the tub and lifts her ass higher.

"You look fucking amazing. Now open your legs wider for me, sweetheart."

She does as I ask, and I'm rewarded by the most mesmerizing sight of her soaking wet pussy, pink and swollen with how truly turned on she is, despite her actions. She glances back at me with those burning amber eyes blinking at me, her lips parting with her rushed breaths.

"Keep being such a good girl, and I'll reward you." Then I bury my face between her thighs again and take what's mine. I suck on her lips, tongue fuck her hole, unable to get close enough. I want her all over my face, so I smell and taste only her.

I ravage this gorgeous peach, slurring and licking. Her growing moans only drive me wilder. Her hips rock and she pushes against my face, wanting more and more. Adorable.

So I pull back and get to my feet. "I need to fuck your pussy," I say.

"Please, Stone, yes."

"That's my girl, you're doing so great."

At my words, her body trembles, her pussy lips are plump, her need dripping down the inside of her thighs. I love nothing more than a woman wet from arousal. Begging me for more.

I palm my cock, and the agony of need hurts. My balls are so tight too. I shift to stand closer behind her.

"Do it," she urges me as she waits for me, so open.

I growl, grabbing her hips, my cock finding her juicy slit. I roar and slam into her, her pussy gripping my dick with each thrust. She's so tight... this is fucking heaven. Here I thought I'd take her, but it turns out, she sent me there just as quickly.

She's moaning, rocking her hips back and forth to meet each of my thrusts. I hammer into her hard and fast, claiming her. And just as her cries grow wilder, my own climax builds, I pull out of her. Much to her anger as she straightens and turns on me with a frown, fire in her eyes. Her tits bounce; they are spectacular.

"What the hell? I was so close," she snaps.

"I know," I smirk, and I reach out and grab her by the back of her neck, roughly hauling her against me. "Come here. I want to watch your face when you scream." My hands glide down the back of her leg, and

I lift it, placing it around my hip, opening her up for me.

My dick slides between her folds, and she's pivoting her hips to accept me, to swallow me. Her eyes roll back in euphoria, her hands clutching my arms. I guide myself into her, then wrap her other leg around me, and I slide completely into her where I belong. I grunt, my hips already stuttering in and out of her.

She's making these hot noises as I thrust into her little cunt because I have no control, and I've been waiting so long. I growl, my body tensing, my balls so damn tight they might have gone up into me.

That's when movement out the corner of my eye catches my attention. I turn to find a man, maybe in his thirties, opening the door and freezing on the spot in shock. The look of pure arousal covers his face as he realizes this might be the luckiest moment of his pathetic life... seeing me fuck my queen.

He stands there, enjoying the show, and I keep on plunging into my babe.

When she realizes we are being watched, she gasps and tries to move, but I hold her in place, taking her harder. "You're not going anywhere," I mutter to her. Then I swing my attention to the pervert. "And you!

Get the fuck out of here before I shove your cock up your ass. Oh, and shut the door behind you."

He rushes out, slamming the door shut.

"How could you let that man watch us?" she whispers between gasps.

"It didn't turn you on?" I ask.

She shrugs.

"Thought so." Then I fuck her hard, take her, returning to where we'd left off. Her breasts rub against my chest as she rides me, her arms looped around my neck. A man could easily lose himself to a girl like Narah... if I hadn't already done so.

Heat ignites between us.

"You'll take it like the good girl you are."

At my words, she suddenly screams, her body quivering, and that sweet pussy strangles my cock. She brings me the most delicious agony, while my heart beats in my chest like a drum and my own orgasm hits me. It comes so hard; it rocks through me, my erection swelling inside her tight little core. I roar with the pressure of her being so small, but it's everything I demand... she is everything to me.

Her orgasm sends me over the edge and I growl as I burst inside of her, flooding her with my seed, pumping. I hold her, both of us, on a different plane. Nothing but pure elation.

I don't even know how long I've been floating. I finally open my eyes, and my cock is deeply embedded in her, knotted, still jerking seed into her. And I find her smiling at me.

My heart bangs in response at how she makes me feel. How the smallest reaction has me falling deeper.

"Good girl, and just so you know, you're all mine."

She laughs, gripping me as I kneel slowly, then take a seat in the tub with my back against the side. Narah straddling my lap, both of us connected, and to have my knot in her, to force us together, is all I've wanted.

"I keep hearing that from each of you guys. But, I mean, you can't all own me?"

I kiss her for the first time tonight, claiming her mouth, licking her lips. "Why not? Back in Denmark, sharing a mate is not uncommon, especially when Omegas are so scarce."

"Makes sense, but also leaves me feeling greedy. To have four of you is nothing I ever expected."

"And finding a girl like you is nothing I ever dreamed of, but here I am fucking you and telling you that you're mine. That you're such a good girl, and I'll take you over and over."

She blinks at me. "You wanna hear something strange?"

"Go for it."

"I don't know why, but I really get turned on when you say that stuff to me about being a good girl."

I laugh. "Oh, I can tell, babe. You have a little kink for receiving praises, and it's fucking hot."

Her mouth partly falls open. "Is that even a thing?"

"Sure is, and I love saying those things to you. It drives me nuts."

I adore this girl so much. She settles against my chest; she rests her cheek in the curve of my neck and her soft breath flares across my skin.

"Tell me about yourself," she says.

"Sure, what do you want to know?"

"Anything and everything."

I settle back, my arms around her, holding her close. "I grew up in a household that was constantly at war. If my father wasn't arguing with my mother, he was beating me. So I spent as little time as I could there."

"Where'd you go?"

"Mostly, Ragnar's house, since he's my cousin. Plus, their home is a mansion compared to everyone else's home, and they had rooms to spare for nights I didn't want to leave. Not that it was calmer there... Ragnar's father is the Alpha of the Ulv Wolves, and a bastard as much as my dad. Once Nikos moved in with Ragnar's family, the three of us bonded quickly and would do anything to get away from wolf politics." I shrug. "We did a lot of hunting in the woods and went away for weeks at a time to escape the pack."

"I'm so sorry. My father was the most amazing man, treating me and my sisters like we were his world. But the Storm Wolves Alpha killed him, blaming him for my mother escaping, then nothing ever felt right again." She falls quiet after that and wraps her arms around my middle.

"Anyway," she says after a little while, "let's not talk about depressing shit." She traces her finger around the inked runes on my chest. "Tell me more about these. What can your magic do?"

"There is magic on my mother's side of the family; they can tap into the power of runes. At the age of five, my mother had them inked on my skin along with a ritual to open me up to elemental magic."

"Wow, that's really young."

"They say the younger you are, the stronger the power. Though, I'm not so sure about that. It took me years to learn the basics of just getting a plant to fold over. Even then, it's nothing compared to what you can do."

She scoffs. "What I saw you do in the Poisonous Forest was not nothing."

"You're too sweet to me." And I steal a kiss. When she moves, her muscles constrict around my cock, and it only awakens the excitement. I doubt I'll ever have a limp dick again.

She smirks at me and squeezes her pussy around my cock again.

"Oh, be very careful, sweetheart, because you're about to raise hell, and I'm ready to go all night."

She sticks her tongue out at me, teasing, and in her eyes, she's begging for more.

"Narah," Ragnar calls my name the moment I step out of the communal mess hall after filling up on porridge. It's a larger cabin than the rest of the buildings in the pack compound. Jae is still inside with two girls she's made friends with. They are similar in age, and it warms my heart to have my sister smile and laugh for a change. She's been forced to grow up too quickly, so if I can give her a few days without worry, then I'll do it.

The raucous voices behind me in the mess hall booms, and I'd almost forgotten how secure it feels to be part of a pack, knowing you are never alone to face whatever this world throws at you.

Ragnar is sauntering past other cabins and coming my way, his mouth widening into a grin like he's got a secret he's about to share. He's wearing cargo pants, combat boots, and a V-neck, short-sleeved tee. Everything about this man is dangerous and handsome.

Guilt turns in my gut after what Stone and I did last night in the baths, but to be fair, the way I am drawn to each of these men is unlike anything I've ever felt. It's different from the attraction I had to Martell—that was purely animalistic and my wolf driving me. Except, what these four Viking Alphas do to me is on another planet. They arouse me with a single word. They make me care for them, and they look out for me. The only people to have done that for me before had been my family.

I feel myself slipping deeper for each of these four men, and with each passing day, the knot of guilt in my chest tightens. I need to speak to Ragnar about this and tell him about my attraction. Even if I don't know if my future will be with them, I need to be honest.

"Morning, little fox." Ragnar takes my hand in his, our fingers interlaced, and he draws me into a stroll.

I swallow the words I want to tell him, unable to voice them right now... at least, so his beautiful smile doesn't fade away. "Someone's in a good mood today," I say instead.

"I might have found a solution to tracking down your mother."

"What? Are you kidding me?" I pause, then I'm throwing myself at him, embracing him.

His powerful arms wrap around me, and he kisses my brow. "There's a seer in town who's agreed to help us."

I pull back, staring at him, completely blank on what to say.

"We should be ready to head out later today," he continues. "Nikos is up and about, his wound almost healed."

"Thank you," I gasp, still lost for breath, that this might be the solution. "This means everything." I pray my mother isn't as dangerous as Kaira implied. I don't even let myself go there with my thoughts. This has to work because, otherwise, I don't know how we're going to get my sister from the witches or eradicate our curse.

He urges me with our linked hands to walk again. "The seer agreed to speak with you this morning and try to find your mother."

"Okay, I'm ready. I don't know what to expect, but I'm assuming it's some kind of reading?"

We come to a stop outside the wooden cabin we'd gone into on our first night of arrival, where the pack Alpha lives, and I glance up at Ragnar, my brow pinching.

"She's waiting for you inside." He pushes open the door.

"She?" And when I turn to look inside, I find Lyssa sitting at the table in their kitchen, waving. She's got her blonde hair pulled tight in a ponytail and wearing a navy-blue hoodie and jeans.

"Hey, Ragnar," she purrs, not even acknowledging me, batting her eyes at him.

I want to roll mine, but instead, I whisper to Ragnar, "Are you sure you got this right?"

He's half-smiling like I made a joke. "Yes, now go." Then he nudges me in the back, and I stumble inside. The door shuts behind me, and I just stand there awkwardly. Silence. Lyssa watching me. The strange smell of burning herbs. I nervously fiddle with my gloves, wishing this was anyone but her.

"If you don't want to do this, that's fine," she snaps, curling her hand around her ponytail as she starts to get up.

Except, if Ragnar is right, then who the hell cares who the seer is, right? As long as I get my answer.

"You're a seer?" I ask and close the distance between us, sliding into the seat across the table from her. She sits back down.

There are two items placed between us. A blade and a small drawstring pouch the color of night. I eye the weapon, not too happy about what that might mean. I'm really not into sacrifices.

"Some call me that, but really it's just an ability from my mother's family. All the women in her bloodline have a touch of divination. She used to have visions of the future, while I can sometimes find lost things."

Part of me toys with asking her more about her mom's ability, considering my vision with my sisters still baffles me. In truth, it terrifies the hell out of me that it portrays a future that will devastate me.

"But tell me something, how did you lose your mother?" she asks, looking at me with her head tilted to the side like I'm a complete moron and somehow misplaced a parent.

I slump back in my chair, not falling for the jab. "She left one day and never came back."

Lyssa watches me as she empties the small bag onto the table. Half a dozen black and gray stones roll out. All of different sizes and shapes. There are no markings on them. They could just be regular pebbles from the garden, for all I know.

"Ever think she doesn't want to be found, then?" She quirks a thin eyebrow. "Sometimes when someone's energy is hiding, I can't see them."

"There has to be a reason she left, and I need to find out," I answer, not intending to give Lyssa any more information. Did I mention I don't trust the girl?

"Give me your hand," she says and places hers on the table, palm side up.

I look down at my hands in my lap, at the sandy-colored gloves I'm wearing, and how this isn't going to work. Maybe this was a mistake after all? Mother... the word wells in my mind like a heavy stone. For years, I've dreamed of finding my mother, and this is my chance, but I don't feel comfortable showing Lyssa what I am.

"Is there another way?" I ask.

She blinks, her brow furrowing. "What do you mean? I just need your hand. I'm not going to chop it off."

Her direct aggression always annoys me. "It's just that..."

"Are we doing this, or are you wasting my time?"

I swallow loudly and start pulling the glove off one hand, nerves twisting in the pit of my stomach. Tensing, I slowly lift my hand with my fingers stained black from under the table, and I wait for her comment.

She gasps, then studies me with her narrowing gaze. "What happened?"

"I upset some witches," I murmur, lying through my teeth.

She's silent for a while, then scoffs. "Yeah, I'd believe that. You are annoying." Then she grabs my hand and puts it palm up on top of hers, studying the lines.

My throat is parched. I'm surprised she says nothing more, seeing as it's more common for witches to have black fingers, just as my mother had. Perhaps Lyssa believes me for real... or she doesn't, and this will come back to bite me in the ass.

"I know you have a thing for Ragnar," she mutters suddenly, catching me off guard.

My spine stiffens, and I go to pull my hand back, but she grasps it hard. "I don't blame you. He's the ultimate Alpha, you know, and I haven't seen what he carries in his pants." She smirks. "But I bet it's going to be huge, and we're going to make so many babies."

Heat burns across my chest at her words. "Look, I didn't come here to talk about your obsession withRagnar."

She barks a laugh. "You believe that's what's going on?" Her fingers dig into the side of my hand, and I swallow the pain. "Do you think you are somehow special just because you're family or whatever lie he made up? I've seen the way you watch him, how he watches you possessively. No family members look at each other that way." Her hand constricts mine further, and I clench my teeth. Her nails are like blades going into my skin. "So, tell me the truth. What the hell have you been doing with my fiancé?"

I breathe faster, everything in my mind pulsing with the banging of my heart. My mind races for a reason she'll believe. Bitter jealousy can make even the most reasonable person paranoid as hell.

"I don't know what you're talking about," I say calmly, trying to pull my hand free, even if it feels like she's ripping it off. But a fiery anger brews in my gut from her hurting me, and I can't help myself. "Maybe the real issue is that Ragnar is not that into you."

A harried wildness flares behind her eyes. Next thing I know, she's gripping the knife from the table and slashing the blade across my palm before I can even react.

Pain explodes, and I scream, pulling backward, but she's holding on with an iron grip. "Hold still, you'll survive," she growls. The knife drops from her hand and hits the table with a thump. Then she takes the stones and places them into my bloody palm.

The sharp pain has me jumping each time the stones hit my wound, and I wince at how badly it hurts.

Then she turns my hand sideways and all the stones tumble onto the table, stained with my blood.

I'm finally able to yank back from her and cradle my hand. "You're fucking crazy, you know that?"

She gets to her feet and grabs a kitchen towel from the counter before throwing it in my face. "I don't like you for going after my man. But I understand. He's a pack leader, and when he rules Savage Sector, you want to be safe. Just like the rest of us."

Her words don't carry venom, but a sense of pity for me. If she knew the truth, she'd be clawing my face off.

She takes a seat back at the table and crosses her legs. "You're lucky Ragnar's helping you, but don't get any ideas. He's got his pack, go choose one of those men."

I blink at her, holding back the crazy laugh in my head at how I'm struggling to accept that I am attracted to all four of the Alphas. I wrap my bleeding hand in the kitchen towel to distract myself.

Lyssa studies the stones on the table, and I start to wonder if she really is a seer or pretended just to warn me off Ragnar.

"Narah, there's someone for everyone out there, and perhaps the person for you is a Beta. Have you ever considered that? Not everyone can be with the best."

"What are you talking about? Omegas can't mate with Betas." As my mother once told me, Alphas lead. Omegas are for rutting and making babies. While Betas are the fighters, the work dogs of the packs, they can't get an Omega pregnant. Only Alphas can.

She shrugs like she knew this all along, but used it to mock me. I really dislike her, even knowing she'll be devastated when Ragnar rejects her.

"Do you even know what you're doing with the divination, or are you wasting my time?" I ask, tucking the kitchen towel corner under the wrapped part, so it doesn't unravel.

"Hush," she says, leaning closer to the scattered stones covered in my blood. Then she glances up at me. "Don't be angry with me. Be angry with the shitty world and with the Alphas who rule it. I know you're trying to survive, I get it."

"Don't patronize me, Lyssa. You say you're going to help me, but all you've done is slice up my hand, then insult me. You know nothing about my past or my issues, so don't pretend you do while you're living safely in this perfect pack protected by your father."

I'm shaking at how angry she's got me.

She reels back in her seat, eyes narrowing. "You want to know the truth? Fine, I'll tell you." Her voice turns dark. "My father deemed me too old to sell to any of the nearby packs for their Alpha leaders. And those neighboring Alphas are all in their sixties or older, and they only want girls the age of your sister. So, then my father decided he was going to give me to the men in this pack as a reward for doing a good job. To share me as they pleased because we don't have enough females." Her words tremble now, and my heart clenches. "I am nothing to my father. I'm a pebble in his shoe. So, when Ragnar came and agreed to claim me, he saved me. I jumped at the chance to escape." Her chin is quivering as she blinks the tears away.

I deflate in my seat and feel like the worst person in the world.

"Lyssa, I didn't know." I reach over to her, but she rears back. "Don't give me pity, just your understanding that I'm doing anything I can to survive and not end up as a sex slave to those desperate men out there. I had nothing, and Ragnar gave me something to hold on to."

I sink in my seat, tears welling in my eyes. The ache that rips through my chest has me close to choking on my breaths. I've been so distracted by my problems, that I just assumed the worst of Lyssa.

"Forgive me for my words," I say softly.

She shrugs and sniffles, then glances down to the stones. "I can see where your mother is."

I straighten in my chair, my heart fluttering like crazy. Mother's alive! "You can? Where?"

She's pointing at two stones next to each other, which means nothing to me.

"I'm going to need a bit more information," I say.

"The Wolf Mountains," she replies with a yawn. "Your mother is there, nestled between them in the valley."

I know exactly where that is... well, I've never been there, as it's far, but the Wolf Mountains overlook a big section of the Savage Sector. I want to yell with excitement, but I'm also torn about Lyssa's predicament. I just hope she's not lying about my mother.

Lyssa gets up from the table and sweeps the stones into her hand before dumping them into the sink, where they clang against the metal.

"You can go now."

I'm on my feet. "Thank you for your help, and for telling me about your situation. Us females are treated like garbage by so many men, so we should look out for one another more. I promise I'll do what I can to help you."

She half-smiles at me over her shoulder. "Just stay away from my man, and all will be fine."

My stomach cramps up because I can't promise that when I know he doesn't want her. I turn on my heel and walk out, needing desperately to speak to Ragnar.

16

NARAH

As soon as I step into our cabin, I find Stone stuffing his clothes into a backpack. "Where's Ragnar?" I ask, looking around for any sign of Jae or Nikos. Nothing.

Stone glances up at me, his eyes smiling. "Morning, sweetheart. He's waiting for us down by the horses with the rest of them. We're leaving."

"Now?"

He nods and drops everything to make his way over to me. His hands instantly cup the sides of my face, and he kisses me in a way that makes me almost forget what I wanted to speak to Ragnar about. My toes curl in my boots, and I return the passion he showered me with last night, parting his lips, taking his tongue into my mouth. And suddenly, I'm back in the baths thinking about how he ravaged me, leaving me begging for more.

When he finally breaks from me, and I find myself leaning in for more, he says, "Jae's packed your belongings. We should go before they send a search party for us. I was supposed to collect you, but had to grab my stuff first." He goes to get his bag and throws it over his shoulder.

That's when I notice Jae's bag is still in the room, along with her coat and her heavy boots. The urgency to see her flares through me. I've lost her twice, and I don't plan on doing so again.

Stone crosses the room to open the door. "After you, my queen." He sweeps his hand for me to exit the cabin.

His words leave me giddy because no one has ever called me that. I won't lie; I love the sound of it. "Thanks." I step outside and quickly cross the lawn toward the stone steps leading out of the village.

"I hear you may know where your mother is," Stone mentions as he shuts the door and follows me.

"Where did you hear that? I just finished talking with Lyssa?"

"Ragnar," he answers and catches up to me. "He's convinced you'll know the answer and has already arranged for our departure from the pack to find her."

"Oh, okay. What if that hadn't been the case?"

"But Lyssa did tell you, didn't she?" he asks with an arch of his eyebrow.

I nod. "The Wolf Mountains."

"Then he was right."

The confidence they hold in Ragnar is incredible.

"So you knew Lyssa is a seer?"

"Yep, and she's completely obsessed with Ragnar."

"Yeah, well, there's a story behind everything, before you judge too quickly."

He glances at me with narrow eyes. "Where's that coming from? The other day, you looked ready to murder the girl for flirting with Ragnar."

"Well, that's because I didn't know the full story." He takes my hand as we saunter past several locals who only stare at us in silence. I use the walk to give Stone a quick summary of my chat with Lyssa and the shitty situation she's in.

"Fuck me, I had no clue, and I bet neither did Ragnar." He squeezes my hand slightly and draws me closer in a protective manner that's really growing on me.

"Whatever happens, we need to help her."

"We will," he assures me and lifts his head as we rush down the main steps from the village.

It's only when we reach the bottom of the stairs that I spot the rest of our gang and my sister, along with Mihai and a group of his men. Everyone's here, including our four horses. The pack Alpha is talking to Ragnar, his arms flailing about as if he's proving a big point.

Jae is waving at me to join her. We walk over. "Thanks for grabbing my things, sis."

"Always got your back." She smirks.

"But why is your stuff still in the cabin?"

"You see, when I spoke to Ragnar, he suggested it might be safer if I stay behind, and I'm going to move in with my new friends until you return. They're sisters, and their mother is super kind to me. Plus, Ragnar made the Alpha swear to keep me protected, or he'll personally hunt him down if anything happens to me."

Unease rolls through me. Being slightly annoyed that she asked Ragnar not me, I say, "It's just that I said I wasn't going to leave you behind again. Thought we'd stick together from now on." I push her hair behind an ear.

She hugs me, and I loop my arms around her, not wanting to be far from her. "Can I be honest with you?" she whispers and draws me away from the group while Ragnar and the Alpha are still talking.

"What's going on?"

Her shoulders drop when she looks up at me, and her arms hang slack at her sides. "Narah, please don't hate me. I do want to find our mother, but I'm also scared of what you'll discover. For so long, it's been easier to tell myself after she left us, she was killed. But what if she left us on purpose? What if..." her voice trails off, and she glances down.

"First, I could never hate you, and second, don't even think that," I say as her hitched breaths sting me. The same doubt has haunted me from the day Mother left us with the Storm Wolves. But having my youngest sister struggle with such fear rips me to shreds.

Lyssa's words return to me... *Ever think she doesn't want to be found?*

What if Mother doesn't want to see us? What if Kaira was right, and she's a danger to us?

I stare at Jae, and my heart cracks at her agony, while she bats away the tears glinting in her eyes. I swallow the heaviness claiming me, and in front of Jae, I try never to show my fear.

I lift her chin with my fingers. "Listen to me. She left us because she had no choice."

She shrugs, her mouth pinching to the side, staring down at her empty hands. "I want to stay here until you return. I'm tired of being scared and running."

Her words rattle me, and my eyes prick. "Oh, Jae." I hug her, wrapping her up in my arms. "Of course. If that's what you want, that's fine."

She doesn't move for a long time, and my heart hammers at the tremor in her voice. How can I make her join us after what she's been through? In the last couple of days, I've seen my younger sister again. Youthful. Happy. Excited about life.

And as much as it kills me, the best thing I can do for her is give her what she needs.

I kick myself for not being the one to acknowledge this. I guess I was too selfish, I wanted her close to me, so I can keep her safe, but it's not about what I want. She has to find her happiness.

"Please stay safe, and don't trust anyone." I reach down to my boot and pull out the small blade I always keep with me, handing it to her. "Anyone comes to hurt you, you stab them in the throat or eye. Then run."

Her gaze softens, filling with an inner glow. "You know, I *can* look after myself, but I'll take the knife." She hastily accepts it and tucks it away into the back of her pants.

"Are we ready to go, Narah?" Ragnar asks from behind me.

I meet his serious gaze and nod. My men climb up on their horses. I give Jae one more hug, wishing I could keep her safe for eternity. Protected from this horrible world, but not sure if I can do that forever.

"You're suffocating me," she chokes out, then laughs. "You better go."

"I know. Love you."

"Love you too."

I release her as her two friends approach her, and Jae's already giggling with them. She'll be safe, I tell myself. She has to be.

When I turn toward my men, it's Stone up on his black horse waiting for me to join him while the other three are riding toward the front gate.

I accept his outstretched hand, and I'm pulled up onto the horse behind him, where I clasp my arms around his middle.

"You ready to go, sweetheart?"

"Yes, and no."

He pats my hands and nudges his horse, then we are trotting after the others. I take a quick glance back and blow Jae a kiss.

"I told Ragnar about your reading with Lyssa," he tells me. "And he got instructions on the quickest way to the Wolf Mountains from Mihai."

"Thank you." I press my cheek to his back, my throat choking up about leaving Jae behind and about our mission.

"Now hold on," Stone instructs. "We're going to try to reach the mountains today. Mihai believes it should only take us a few hours."

Please, Moon Goddess, let everything go smoothly for a change. Please.

A few hours have morphed into half a day, and we're only just approaching the mountains. Right now, we've come to a stop near a river that leads us directly to the valley between the Wolf Mountains. They're monstrous and tower over us, the sun close to vanishing behind their peaks. The horses are grazing in the pasture behind me. Beyond that, the field seems to have grown out of control with what looks like tall corn stalks. I've already told the guys we're collecting a bunch before we leave.

Crius is lying flat on his back next to me, his hands behind his head, and he's got a long grass stalk sticking out of his mouth. He glances over at me, squinting against the sunlight. "You know if it wasn't for the rogue wolves, the zombies, and the constant war over land, this might be a decent world to live in."

I take a seat next to him in the grass, staring out at Stone and Ragnar chatting by the river, at least twenty feet away. Nikos isn't too far from them, still eating the rest of the cold stew we'd brought from town. I don't blame him... he's a huge guy, and he's healing, so if he eats all our food, so be it.

"The old world must have been incredible," I reply to Crius. "Like, can you imagine each person having a car to get around? I bet they were nothing like the rust bucket I've seen my old Alpha drive."

"If it was me, I'd get a Harley-Davidson. Been reading about them since before I grew up, and it's been a dream," Crius says, and I smile, meeting his gaze. "Something about them gives me a hard-on." He chuckles to himself.

When I don't reply, he asks, "What? You got a strange look on your face."

I twist around to face him, drawing a bent leg between us. "That's probably the first time you just sounded... normal."

He eyes me, then pushes upright to a sitting position. "Normal? Getting hard over a bike? What have I been before this? A crazed lunatic?"

I half-laugh, gaining myself a raised eyebrow, but I shrug. "You're usually acting all macho, telling the guys you're better than them, but it's nice to have more of this side of you. Where I get to see what you like and how much bikes turn you on." I stick my tongue out at him.

He smirks, studying me like he's trying to read my thoughts. There's something dangerously addictive about having these wolves' attention on me.

They're an obsession. And I always want more, like I can't get enough.

"What?" I gape.

"You're cute in the things that you find fascinating about me. There aren't that many happy memories from my childhood, and I'm happy to share those with you if it keeps you smiling."

"Now you're teasing me," I say. "Of course, I want to know more about you."

He leans toward me, eyebrows furrowing. "Are you being serious right now, or are you fucking with me?"

"Why are you so shocked?"

Crius pulls back and folds his arms over his bent knees. "Because no one ever asks me about my past. They're just the ugly, broken memories."

My pulse spikes and I reach over, placing a hand on his arm. "I'm not like everyone else. I mean, how messed up is my life? My fated mate tried to kill me, my mother might have run out on me, my sister sided with witches, and on top of everything, I still have no idea how to properly control my magic. Now, that is fucked up." I leave out the part where I'm falling for four men, and my heart is slowly tearing apart, wondering how I'm supposed to deal with that.

He scoffs, turning his gaze to the river ahead of us when he speaks. "I'll do you one better. I killed my brother, and it wasn't an accident. And he was the greatest brother in the world."

My breath hitches and might have stopped briefly as I process his words. I'm searching my brain for any response, any kind of comfort, but I'm stumped. I want to desperately ask him why, but I don't think he wants to tell me until he's ready.

I just squeeze his hand slightly. "I'm sorry."

"Nothing to be sorry about," he groans, and I feel his arm tensing. "I did it, and my time is coming." He abruptly pushes to his feet and marches down to the river.

A sinking feeling in my stomach has me drowning. What did Crius mean by 'his time is coming'? What happened between him and his brother?

It's like every time I check under a rock, something dangerous bites me, and with so much weighing down on me, I'm struggling to not worry about every freaking person I've crossed paths with.

I regret saying anything to Crius.

A frigid cold swishes across my arms, and I hug myself.

Mother comes to mind again, as she has for most of the trip.

Will she bundle me in her arms or pretend she doesn't know me? It's been so long since she left us with the Storm Wolves that she might have forgotten what I look like. Am I ready to face her after Father was murdered, and I blamed her for leaving us?

My knuckles turn white from how hard I'm curling them into fists; at the dread of what to expect, terrified she'll hate me.

A horse neighs behind us, the sound almost startling, followed by the other mares. I twist around to watch all four horses bolting right into the wild cornfield, vanishing from sight.

I'm on my feet in seconds, as is Nikos. "The horses," I call out, but when I turn back to the other three men, the blood in my veins turns to ice.

They're racing my way, panic scribbled over their faces. And from across the river, a swarm of undead is plunging into the water, scrambling right in our direction.

I shudder, my heart thundering like a storm.

Fuck. Fuck. Fuck.

"Run," Nikos bellows, already yanking his shirt off. "Change into your wolf. We'll be faster." He's yelling his orders at me while my gaze is glued to the sheer number of creatures scrambling up on our side of the river. They rush awkwardly, stumbling, but they're fast.

Fear strangles me, and I can barely draw breath into my lungs. We're in an open field. No trees to try to climb, nothing but land. We are so fucked.

My skin crawls at the way they rasp, their teeth clattering, arms reaching out for us. Their inhuman sounds leave me trembling. Torn clothes, hands of skin and bones, broken limbs, missing skin.

I recoil, my stomach rolling, and unable to even think straight. There are so many.

"Narah, get fucking running," Ragnar yells. He's thundering toward me while the others are all transforming.

I spin and run, my feet hitting the ground hard. Panic slams into me. I burst into the field of corn, and only then do I notice something dark shifting through the stalks on my left. Something else is in here with us.

My thoughts fly to the horses... except the shadows rushing about are not that big.

Figures are shoving through the long stalks. The sound of teeth gnashing carries on the wind, and the vibration of magic races through my veins. My legs pump, my boots striking the ground as I shove past the corn.

There's movement from my right, and one of the undead is coming so fast and unexpected that a cry spills past my lips.

I raise my hands, magic tingling across my skin, when Ragnar crashes through the field like a truck. "Run!" He's still in human form, and when I whip around, I trip on something. I hit the ground hard on my knees, and I scramble to get back up.

Ragnar has my arm, and I'm flying forward before I know it, out of reach of the creature. The Alpha grips my arm and hauls me alongside him.

All around us, the stalks are shaking, shadows everywhere. And then I see one monster amid the corn stalks. It has an empty eye socket, sunken cheeks, and lips long ago worn away.

My skin crawls.

"You need to transform, you'll be faster." Ragnar's words race as fast as he runs with me by his side. We sprint, and the other three men have already taken their wolf forms, sticking close to us.

It takes moments for me to stop being so freaked out, and I call my wolf forward. But just as I do that, an undead with only one arm bursts toward us, right in our path. The dislocated bony jaw that half hangs from his face makes me sick.

Ragnar roughly wrenches me out of the monster's path.

My head swings left and right. Fear is surging through me at how fast things went bad.

Another comes at us quickly, and the five of us gather together. Crius charges at an undead. He slams into the thing, bringing it down fast, then flinches back, not even wanting to bite into the decayed flesh. I can't blame him.

But when more figures arrive, my worst nightmare comes to life. Shadows crowd in around us, their groans and clacking teeth like a song of death. There are so many of them... I lift my hands, needing to draw on my energy, no matter the risks.

Stone shifts back to human form instantly. He's naked and kneels, slapping his palm to the ground as he calls to his magic, having the same thought as me. Power licks along my skin, and the sensation brings my own power forward, stronger.

Two creatures burst out of the field and attack him.

I scream, lunging to help him.

But Ragnar charges at the monsters quicker, as does Stone.

Angry power flares through me in waves, biting into my skin. I'm shaking, but for a change, I don't try to stop the surge. Instead, I throw my arms out into the field, picturing my power hitting every last zombie, tearing them apart.

I funnel my thoughts into the undead, into my magic, into somehow gaining some control of my power.

Power shoots through me in a cruel, painful snap, throttling me at the core. White electricity spikes out of my hands, forking in a dozen directions from both hands. It zigzags uncontrollably through the field. It's hard to tell if it's working when all I hear are the men behind me shouting something and the monsters surrounding us groaning and clattering their teeth.

A sharp ache digs into my chest, deepening the longer I draw on magic.

That's when I notice the creatures that came for Stone now convulsing on the ground, my white lines of power skewed through their chests. Something lofty catches my attention from behind me, and I whip around.

Stone has built an enclosure around him and the men made of twisted roots pushing up from the earth, completely encasing them in a dome.

But my magic strikes his protection regardless of what I intended, turning the roots it touches to ash. Holes punch through the structure, and looking back at me through them are my men with terrified eyes.

They're scared of me! That hurts a lot.

The burned smell of my attack intensifies, and only when I look down do I notice that the black stains on my finger have spread up to my knuckles.

Panic has me screaming, and I flinch back, shaking my hands. The magic fades instantly, just like the world around me.

I fall and hit the ground, completely lost.

A soft touch strokes my cheek, waking me, and the memories fill me. Of undead attacking us in the field. Me falling over and passing out. My wolves being in danger.

My heart thunders loudly in my ears, the terror swallowing me. A cry spills from my throat, and I scramble to my feet, magic already crackling over my fingers.

"Whoa," Crius cries out, recoiling from me.

But a burst of my power already shoots across the room and strikes the white wall of the room I'm in, burning a hole right through the painted stone.

"Narah!" Crius' voice booms, and just as quick, the power rushing from my hand flatlines.

I stumble on the bed I'm standing on, gasping for air, trying to understand what's going on. "W-Where am I?"

My head spins because I'm no longer in the field but in a strange room.

Crius' face has blanched as he stares up at me. "Nothing's going to harm you," he says, offering me his hand. "You're safe. So, you wanna come down from there, magic girl?"

I don't move at first, still waiting for my thoughts to catch up, for the sleep to fade from my eyes.

"What's going on?" I gasp.

I accept Crius' hand, and he helps me down.

"We're at a small inn in the mountains. The undead are no longer a threat, and you are with me." He studies me, searching my face and body like I might have injuries. "Are you hurt?"

I shake my head, hating how disorienting it is to wake up here when my mind is still buzzing from the attack in the field. And from not understanding what happened.

I glance down at the blue tee I'm wearing that's wrinkled and falls halfway down my thighs. It hangs off a shoulder, and I assume belongs to one of the guys.

"Did you undress me?" I reach down and feel through the shirt that at least I've still got my underwear on.

He grins at me. "Don't worry, I didn't strip you completely, even if I was tempted. But I will admit, I did squeeze your tits."

"Wow, you groped me while I was unconscious." I'm not too sure how I feel about that.

He shrugs. "I'm not passing up the opportunity when I've been dying to do it. Your body is fucking stunning. And you will be mine soon enough." His voice darkens, and I have no doubt he means every word. "Plus, I give you permission to do anything you desire to me anytime I am sleeping or passed out." He winks.

"Well, how about going forward, no one gropes anyone unless they're awake?"

He shrugs, and I can't tell if he agrees or not.

Plus, I'm not sure if I should be blushing or slapping him. Instead, I push the thoughts aside and glance around the room at the wooden bed and bedside table. At the burned hole in the wall still smoking, and the acrid smell lingering. Shit. There's not much else in here, but I see the blue sky outside through the glass door to the balcony.

"Where exactly are we, Crius? What happened after we were attacked? Where are the rest of the guys?" My confusion hurts my head, and I hate not knowing what's going on.

"Everyone is safe. You are safe." He crosses the room and opens the glass door to the small balcony. A gust of fresh, cool air rushes inside and whooshes through my hair. "How about I show you?"

His eyebrow arches as he beckons me to join him, so I step forward.

Out on the balcony, I glance down at the enormous expanse of land stretching out as far as the eye can see. And woods in every direction.

"That's where we came from, isn't it?" I point ahead.

"Yep. Now, lower your gaze, gorgeous." Crius places a hand across my back, and I grip onto the metal railing as I do so. It's a long-distance down, making my stomach queasy. There are trees all around us like we're hanging out of a balcony on the side of a cliff.

When my attention drifts to the land at the base of the mountain, the cornfield comes into view. Except, something's odd about it. I lean forward, squinting at the small black patches dotting the entire field.

"What in the world are those?"

"Your beautiful magic," Crius coos. "Those charred spots are where each undead stood the moment your power zapped them out of existence. You burned them to ashes, babe." He turns toward me, but I can't stop staring at how many black markings there are. My pulse races, my breaths coming too quick. There are at least fifty of them... maybe more.

"That's got to be a mistake," I mutter, mostly to myself. This can't be right. The sheer magnitude scares me because how can I control such things?

"Narah, your magic is fucking epic." He throws his arms into the air, making a huge circle with them to exaggerate his point. "I've never heard of a witch doing this. Do you know what this could mean if you gained a better handle on your power?"

His enthusiasm only terrifies me further.

Crius slides an arm around my waist and draws me roughly against him, face to face. "I'll be honest, when I saw what you did, it both scared me and got me fucking hard. You are a powerful witch, Narah, and intimidating. And once we brought you here, I jerked off thinking about how sexy and strong you'd been out there, eradicating those creatures."

I cut him a sharp stare, not even sure what to do with that information. Though, I won't ignore that compliment he gave me. "Did you jerk off while you were groping me?"

He barks a laugh. "Do you think I'm that much of a monster?"

I refuse to answer that right now and instead say, "It has to be some mistake. I don't have that kind of ability."

His eyes widen. "Babe, did you see the carnage you left down there? You did that."

"But what about you and the guys? I didn't know how to stop the magic from attacking you as well."

"Well, that's the risk we take by being with a lethal girl like you... but Stone's magic protected us. Each time your power burned down his shield of knotted roots, he built another. You know what was interesting, though? That even after you passed out, the power kept trickling out of you like you'd generated so much magic, it had to escape your body. I'll be honest, I've never heard of that happening before."

"Goddess, I'm a freak. I never wanted this." I try to pull away from him, but he holds me in place.

"Don't say that shit. You've been given a gift. You just need to learn to manage it, that's all."

I blink at him, his expression serious, and say, "I'm really trying, you know, but until I left the Storm Wolves pack, I hid my ability. My mother taught me almost nothing about using my magic."

"Well, then, lucky that we've reached the Wolf Mountain town. Now, we can start searching for your mother, if this is where she's hiding. But I think you're going to like this place. It's built on the side of a mountain."

I don't even know what to say. I'm still hung up on what my magic did. How is that even possible?

"Wanna go see the rest of the crew? They'll be excited to see you're awake. But I have one request before we go."

"What is it?" I'm not sure I can take any more surprises just yet.

Crius is grinning widely, and even before he asks, I suspect it's going to be something wild, based on the feral look in his gaze. It's not too different from the expression he had when he busted Nikos and me behind the tavern. "Can you promise me that when I fuck you, you're going to tickle me a bit with your magic? What you did out there was just mind-blowing. And I need to feel it." His pale hazel eyes keep me frozen in place as I try to decipher what he's just asked me.

"You want me to hurt you?" I gasp at the words.

The corner of his mouth curls up. "Just a bit, honey."

Well, shit, I was not expecting that, or for his question to send a tingle down my spine with how adamant he was that we'll sleep together. "I mean, I don't want to kill you."

His sexy grin curls his lips once more, then he pushes a stray lock of hair off my face. "We're talking about a small zap," he pants against my mouth. Then he's kissing me, so deeply, so desperately, that I soften against him, convinced our souls have just merged. His lips have me buzzing, and every stroke of his tongue sends a delicious tingle through my body. How is he doing that? I need more, more, more.

My hands reach up and tangle in his dark golden hair. He moves fast, his mouth ravenous, his hands sliding down to my ass, squeezing it, pushing me against his erection.

"I've wanted to kiss you for so long," he murmurs, then dips his mouth to my neck, inhaling my scent. He's licking me in long strokes, sending my whole body into delicious shudders.

He devours my neck as he walks me back up against a wall, all the while kneading my ass in a way that feels so good. His hands roam over my body, fingers pulling at the elastic of my underwear, and in seconds, he has them ripped off me.

Deftly, he brushes his fingers between my thighs, and my entire body heats up. I moan as he teases me, never going high enough to fully satisfy, but driving me insane with lust. His other hand is under my shirt, cupping a breast, pulling at a nipple, and there's nothing gentle about the way he does it. I'm shivering with arousal because I suspect having sex with a man like Crius will be rough and wild and fucking amazing.

I don't even understand how quickly we moved from me almost zapping him, to having him now hump me against the wall. But I notice I'm also not pushing him away.

A loud knock comes at the door, and we freeze.

"If you don't open up, I'm breaking this down," Nikos shouts as he rattles the locked door.

And I can't help but laugh at the irony of Nikos interrupting, just as Crius had outside the tavern.

"I'm going to fucking murder him," Crius whispers against my lips. "Want me to throw him off the balcony? Then I can bring you to the most intense orgasm you'll ever experience."

"He's not going to give up, you know." It's not exactly the ideal situation, considering I still haven't had a chance to talk to Ragnar about my relationship with each of the men.

"I can work with that," Crius admits, and starts kissing my neck again, but I know he'll do something crazy, so I slip out from under his arm and search for my underwear. They're lying on the bed, ripped.

"Crap."

"You don't need them for now." Crius tugs my shirt up and slaps my bare ass. "Though we've bought new clothes, seeing we lost all of ours with the horses. Including some underwear for you."

I moan in the best possible way, then go to the door to stop Nikos' constant banging.

When I open it, the frown he wears morphs into a smile. "Hey, beautiful. It's good to have you back." He grabs me by hand and wraps me in his arms, my cheek pressed to his chest. He's rock hard and radiating heat. Why does it feel so incredible to be in his arms?

"Don't pull that stunt again. It fucking scared the hell out of me when you fainted," he whispers.

"Don't be such a baby," Crius states as he strolls past us. "And Narah, I've found you a new pair of undies."

My cheeks burn up, and I turn to see him swinging my black ones in his hand.

"What the hell?" Nikos growls.

I snatch them from Crius and give him an evil stare. "Seriously?" I quickly step into them and slide them up my legs, both men watching intently, wanting to catch a quick peek. Instead, I turn away from them and flash them my ass before I tug my underwear the rest of the way up.

"So." I face them in the narrow hallway, gripping my hips. "Where the heck are the other two?"

"Sweetheart," Stone calls from behind me, and I twist my head to see him waiting for me from several feet away near another door. "We're over here."

I can't help smiling and rush over the floorboards on bare feet, realizing I should have probably found more clothes to put on, but what's done is done. And I have this feeling that if I return to my room, Nikos and Crius will end up in a fight and someone will go over the balcony.

Stone waves me in and grabs my ass, which I ignore, on the way into a room twice the size of the one I woke up in. It has a separate bedroom and a main room. Fancy.

I meet Ragnar's gaze.

He's on a couch in black pants and a matching shirt, his muscles bulging against his thin fabric. He sits with legs spread wide, an arm across the back of the sofa, and he's huge, taking up a good portion of the seat. "Are you feeling better?" he asks, not moving right away, and is it bad that my first thought is wanting to climb on top of him, straddle his lap, and pin him down, so I can trace all those muscles with my tongue?

I blame Crius, of course, for getting me hot and bothered. Instead, I go and flop down beside him on the sofa. "Confused. Crius showed me the cornfield. It's so freaky and doesn't feel like something I could do." I tuck my legs under me while the other three men hover in the hallway for some reason.

Ragnar's hand cups the side of my face, his thumb running across my lower lip. "There's something very special about you, Narah. And I don't think you're just a witch, which I've said before. What you did out there is extraordinary."

"Yeah, extraordinarily terrifying." I study my hands and how my fingers are now completely black like they've been singed. "This isn't right, is it?"

When I lift my head, he's scanning my hands too. "I've heard it said that magic needs balance. Energy used must be taken from somewhere and then replaced. Stone draws his power from the earth, an abundance, but if he takes too much, it wears him down." Ragnar collects my hand in his. "Maybe with you, it's similar."

I lean into his side, tucking myself under his arm as he wraps it around me.

"Stone told me what Lyssa said to you," he murmurs.

I perk up. "And?"

"And I had no idea of her situation." His brow furrows at his words.

"But you'll fix it, right? Find her somewhere safe to escape."

His response is immediate. "When I take over Savage Sector, yes, but not beforehand. I need Mihai's allegiance."

"Of course." I frown and collapse back against him, knowing that means playing up the pretense of him being her fiancé. It's fake, but it still ignites a viscous flame in my chest. My stomach churns at how desperately Lyssa believed Ragnar was her knight in shining armor, just like in the old human fairy tales I've read.

"Are you jealous, little fox?"

"Ha, you wish." In fact, I am burning up with jealousy, but I keep it to myself.

He laughs. "Like I said before, you are mine and I don't need anyone else. But while we're on the topic, tell me, Narah, what's going on with you and my men?"

I don't move, my heart is racing and my throat is suddenly dry. I should look up and read his expression, but I remain attached to his side. I grew up ingrained with the notion that a woman has one man. That's how soulmates worked. Except this is something else. I've already found my fated mate, and he rejected me.

Blushing, I lick my lips and say, "Sometimes I don't understand my own feelings. Maybe even less than my magic. That's crazy, right?"

He gives no response, and I reluctantly pull back. He's watching me carefully, his face stoic, and it's hard not to be distracted by this handsome man next to me.

"I told myself that I have to find my sisters, and then we go our own way. But then... things started to feel different."

"How so?" he asks evenly.

"When I gave myself to you in the woods, something shifted in me, and I knew then it might have been a mistake going there with you. Now, I can't stop thinking about being with you, and yet I want nothing to do with the war you intend to bring to the Savage Sector."

"War is inevitable to achieve peace."

I huff at his stiff responses and questions. "Stop being so diplomatic and serious. You're freaking me out," I blurt. "Just tell me. Are you pissed that I'm attracted to your men as well as you? Or because I let them fuck me, and that I keep thinking about a ridiculous notion of having four men in my life?" I rub a hand over my chest to soothe the ache settling there from the hard expression sliding on his face.

Then I rub my sweaty palms down my shirt.

"Shit, Narah, do you even know what you've done to me? I share everything with my men, but when I met you, something inside me broke." He pushes to his feet, leaving me on the sofa. "I actually thought this might be my second chance after losing my fated mate. That I might find that one special person for me." He pauses several feet away, standing tall, his arms hanging by his side, while my heart shudders and I can't breathe.

Those pale blue eyes see right through me. Those lips I've craved from the first time they touched me call to me again.

He is gorgeous and protective, and I crave him. But the deep splintering pain in my chest comes from the disappointment on his face, his mouth pressed tight.

"You've been through so much. As we all have," he continues.

I really hate where this is going, even if I had every intention of raising this topic with him. But now backpedaling seems like an amazing idea.

"I thought maybe you might feel the same way after I marked you and our wolves connected." His tone sharpens, and that stony expression slides over his face again.

Getting to my feet, I go over to him, noting the other three guys still in the hallway, and I know they're listening in on our conversation. Maybe it's for the best, as this involves them as well.

"This feels really weird," I say. "I mean, you were my first guy ever. I gave you all of me, and I know zero about men. Yet, around all four of you, something comes to life inside me." I take his hand and place it over my heart. "It's crazy that I'm even standing here, arguing this point, when all I should do is keep my focus on rescuing my sisters, not losing my head and heart. But that's what I seem to be doing. I can't help myself because there's something I need from each of you. Something that I crave, that I'd kill for to keep you all safe. So, I'm not sure what I can say to make you understand."

He sighs and doesn't respond for a long pause. "I should have known that you would rip me apart," he mutters, pulling his hand away, but his words irritate me.

I step after him. "Look, I'm sorry this hasn't gone exactly to your perfect plan. But nothing has gone to my plan either, and I'm making do. I'm sorry I'm drawn not only to you but to your men as well. Trust me, none of this is what I had in mind when I asked for your help with my sisters. But I also need you to know that I don't belong to any of you unless I choose to, and I won't be treated as an object for all four of you to fight over. I'd rather walk away than create a war in your pack."

Silence sticks to me like tar, choking the oxygen right out of my lungs. Heat sears over my face and neck. When had I gotten so brazen to stand up for myself so forcefully?

"For someone with no experience with men, you had no issues fucking mine. So I'd say you know exactly what you're doing," he growls under his breath.

Anger rises through me at his response, at the bitterness in his voice. I never asked to fall for these wolves, but that's my mistake.

"Don't worry," I snap back, my throat constricting, my eyes stinging with tears at his hurtful words. "I hear you loud and clear. I won't ever touch you again. I screwed up by giving you the impression I was only yours." My entire body is shaking. I still hadn't made up my mind about being with all the men, but at the mention of maybe losing one of them, it set my nerves on edge. A possessiveness came over me that he'd stand between me and them. And what he doesn't understand is the length I'd go to for him to stay by my side too. But I can't do this now.

I stomp toward the doorway, shuddering with anger, my eyes pricking. And I'm furious at myself. *Men are monsters. They always hurt you,* Mother used to say, and I never understood what she meant until now. First Martell rips me apart, now Ragnar.

Heavy footsteps hit the floorboards behind me. Next thing I know, Ragnar's hands are on my waist, and he's pushing me around to face him. A feral snarl rips from his throat, a primal animal sound, his wolf prowling behind his eyes. "I understand perfectly well."

I fist my hands and slam them into his chest as he walks me backward. "I hate you for speaking to me that way." A loose tear slips out and rolls down my cheek.

My back crashes into the wall, he grabs my throat, then kisses me so hard that I know it's going to bruise.

"Is this what you crave from all of us?" he asks.

"Fuck you!" But I kiss him back, regardless. Maybe I'm weak because he takes away all my inhibitions and shakes me to my core.

I tilt my head as he drags his lips down my neck. He releases his grasp and roughly tears the shirt down my shoulder. Then he bites into the soft curve of my neck, his teeth tearing skin.

I cry out and throw my head back, closing my eyes as his lips clamp around the bite hard, one hand on my breast, the other gripping my arm, keeping me in place. The feel of him dominating me sends a blanket of arousal through me.

I need him all over me, to take me savagely, but that comes with a price. He will need to share me.

Yet, he wants to inflict pain, to make me hurt for the pain he's feeling. I grab his brown hair, bringing his face up to mine, and our mouths clash in an angry, messy kiss.

"Um, Ragnar?" Nikos calls from the doorway, breaking the thick tension in the room. "There's someone here to see Narah."

I stiffen and break from Ragnar's kiss. My lips already feel puffy and sore when I speak. "Me?"

"Bring them in," Ragnar growls and steps away from me like he knows who's coming, but his eyes never leave mine. "Little fox, we'll finish this later."

I stumble on my feet; the wall catching me, while my heart bleeds as I see the true hunger and possessiveness he has over me. With how much he's struggling to share me with his men. And I don't know how I'm going to fix this.

18

NARAH

A woman steps into Ragnar's room.

The first thing that catches my eye is the teal-colored dress that flutters around her legs with a golden ribbon wrapped around her waist. Hair as dark as the night and cascades over her shoulders, rosy lips smiling with deep creases at the corners of her mouth. But when I look into familiar eyes, I lose all feeling in my body.

They're amber... a mirror image of mine. Just like the high cheekbones, the narrow nose, the way she stands, unsure where to put her hands, so she fidgets with the ribbon and then her hair.

My breath catches in my chest.

I choke on my tears.

"Mamma," I whisper. It's all I can manage as my body shudders. I try to come to terms with who's standing before me, who I had assumed for so long was dead, who I thought about daily, and every small thing she'd ever said to me is imprinted on my mind like a torn map through life.

I cross the room so fast that I'm hugging her in seconds, sobbing hard.

"Narah, I've missed you so much." She embraces me, stroking my hair, and I'm suddenly a child again, desperate for her to tell me everything is going to be alright. That she's here now, and I no longer have to stumble through life like a blind fool.

Somehow she smells just as I remember her... like flour and sugar as if she's been baking something sweet. I squeeze my eyes shut and remember how safe I felt growing up, how she tucked us into bed, told us stories, made sure we never saw the ugly side of life. I miss those times. Which is ridiculous because everyone grows up eventually. Some just do so sooner... like I had to.

When I finally pull back to really look at her, she's wiping her wet eyes too. I can't help but notice how much older she is now. Thinner too, her skin is not as smooth across her neck, but the way she looks at me is the same. It's full of adoration and leaves me feeling loved. All I can think about is how many years I've lost with her, and it's close to impossible to stop the tears.

"I've been waiting for the day when I could finally see you again," she says in her sing-song voice and offers me an awkward smile like she wants me to forget that she left us all alone. "And look at you and how much you've grown. How are Jae and Kaira? I'm sure they are so much taller now." Pain etches on her face as she speaks of us, and it destroys me to hear the quiver in her voice as it's clear she's putting on a brave face.

"Jae's safe for now. We left her with friends and Kaira…" I glance down momentarily. "She's with the witches in the Enchanted Woods who've spelled her."

She sighs heavily. "Ragnar told me about Kaira being used by the witches as leverage to control you, along with the curse they've put on you," she answers softly. "You've all gotten yourself into some mess."

I fumble with the shirt, easing it over the bite mark Ragnar gave me near my neck, wishing I wore something more suitable than a wrinkled men's tee. That's when I glance around the room to notice he's left me alone with my mother, but the door remains open.

"How did you find me?" I ask.

"Your friend, Ragnar, found me. He was asking around for someone to help him with a curse, and it turns out he was looking for me specifically. How did you know I was here?" She walks to the balcony glass door and opens it, letting in a light breeze that flutters through her hair and dress.

I follow her outside. "A seer told me where you'd be."

Her mouth thins like she's not a fan of my response. "I would have found you, eventually."

"Yes, but maybe I need your help now." The way she's almost disappointed that we tracked her down irks me. "Why haven't you come for us? And why did you leave us at the mercy of the Storm Wolves? We were only kids. Even after Father was butchered, you never returned. I was so young and cried every night, terrified." I lick my dry lips and blink back tears, my mind swimming with so many more questions.

"Narah, I'm so sorry you were forced into that. I hate that you and your sisters endured such pain." She pushes loose hair out of my face. "But I didn't have a choice. I made a heart-wrenching decision to protect you three. I don't know if you can forgive me, but I hope one day you will."

"Then tell me, please, so I understand why you abandoned us." Something inside me twists, and I suck in a shaky breath. Suddenly, I imagine I'm back with the Storm Wolves with my sisters. We're kneeling by

Father's grave after he was brutally killed. Our finger-nails were packed with dirt, our hands filthy because no one would help us dig a hole for him, so we did it ourselves and buried our father just outside the pack grounds.

I can't stop shaking. Those memories I've kept hidden for so long now rip through me.

Mother turns toward the field, her hands white-knuck-ling the railing. The wind whips at dress and hair. Yet, I don't feel a thing but the numbness that carries me to a place I've avoided for years, and now I am drowning in the past, in sorrow, in heartache.

"You need to know what you are first," she begins. "We're not witches, Narah. Our bloodline comes from an extremely powerful sorceress. We possess a heredi-tary gift for performing magic that gives us the ability to use unimaginable power."

"Sorceress?" I've only read about them in ancient books, which were mainly fictional stories. And they were mostly just magic users, from what I could gather. "So, what's the difference between that and a witch?"

"Witches cast a spell with objects and sacrifices. They call to the elemental energies around them. But you, my dear," she turns to face me, "you can conjure magic instantly. It's why witches fear us and want us dead. We have the ability to destroy them if given the chance. But that means catching them when they're vulnerable and not shrouded in spells and charms to protect themselves. It's nothing compared to what a sorceress can do."

I lift my hands, staring at my black fingers. "Well, my attempt at magic hasn't exactly gone to plan so far."

"That is because you're drawing power from within you. In desperate times, we may need to pull magic from our souls, but that comes at a price. You're eradicating your life source by using magic this way. It's dangerous—you can never undo the damage."

I blink at her, wanting to cry. I had no idea until now what I'd been doing. "I don't know any other way. You never showed me."

Her gaze softens. "I promise I'll make it up to you. I'll train you how to take energy from those around you, and—"

"Wait... Say that again. You are draining other people to use magic?" A shiver zips up my spine at the thought.

She nods. "Energy doesn't manifest out of thin air, Narah. It must come from somewhere. A sorceress' power lets her take energy from humans, from shifters, from witches, from any living thing. Animals are too small, and you'd hurt them, so I don't recommend that. You don't take enough to kill people, but it will usually knock them out for days or even weeks, depending on how much you deplete them."

There is so much to digest that it still hasn't registered that I'm a sorceress. It doesn't really mean much to me right now.

All I can focus on is where I draw my power.

Her shoulders square, her expression firms. "So, to answer your earlier question, I was found by the local coven while I snuck out one night with your father to catch a wild turkey. The witches caught us, and when I attacked them with the power I drew from your father, it gave me enough energy to kill one of them. The rest ran... but I knew they'd return. They always do, just as they had when they killed my mother and grandmother."

She lowers her gaze, and the grief on her face has me reaching over to take her hand in mine. "It's okay."

"No, it's not. I made a horrible decision I would never wish upon anyone. Stay and protect my three girls, knowing the witches would return in large numbers. Or leave the pack and draw them away from you, well aware that the Alphas would punish your father for losing me. Omegas are too precious to let go," she says sarcastically.

I swallow the lump in my throat and squeeze her hand as a tear slides down her cheek.

"We could have all escaped together," I suggest.

She half-snorts. "And be on the run from rogue wolves and witches with three young Omegas? We wouldn't last long. The Storm Wolves pack was the safest place."

My heart pounds harder at hearing that she knowingly sacrificed Father to save us. I pull back, unable to get enough air into my lungs while bile scrapes the back of my throat. I'm going to be sick, and my head pulses. I've waited so long to know the truth about why she left us, but it hurts so much more than I ever thought.

"I need to sit down for a bit," I murmur and step back inside on wobbly legs, then crash on the couch.

I grab a small cushion and hug it to my chest, rocking on the spot as Mother joins me.

"I don't blame you if you don't forgive me for your father's death, for leaving you and your sisters. At the time, I did what I thought was best for you three. You have always been my priority."

While I remain quiet, my head buzzes with the news of what I am, what it means, and how we can save Kaira.

With it comes the heartache of the past of my father's death, of Mother making the decision that set all our futures into motion. Each time I think about it, I feel sick to my stomach.

"For too long, I stayed away for your own safety, but now it's my turn to fight for you. I have always loved you three and thought about you every day."

"I have so many more questions," I say. "But maybe not right now." I rub my brow where a headache is forming. With it comes me trying to make peace with the past because I hate the excruciating sting burrowing through my heart.

"Of course. But first, let me remove the curse the witches have placed on you and your wolf protectors. How does that sound?"

I perk up, even if I'm wondering where she'll get the power to help. From us? "But will the witches know the curse has been tampered with?"

Her lips pinch to the side. "Depends on how they did the curse and if they linked it to them, so the short answer is, maybe. But I can set a protection barrier around you and the wolves for now. That will stop them from detecting the broken curse."

"That would be perfect." I pause for a bit. "It would have been wonderful to learn all this from you when I was younger, but I know why you didn't."

She smiles tenderly. "At midnight, come to the rear of the village in the woods. Ragnar knows the location. Tonight we will remove the curse, and then we can share a meal together. I will cook your favorite. Chicken stuffed with fruit and nuts."

I half-laugh, half-cry at words I've only dreamed of hearing again. "You remembered."

She crouches in front of me, her hand on my knee. "I have never forgotten. I've cried so many nights over losing my family, so to see you again is like a miracle."

I sniffle, and she gets to her feet.

"Alright, I have lots to prepare then." She clears her throat and pushes her dark hair out of her face. "I will see you and your friends soon." Her grin is bright, and my chest beams with a joy that is tearing me apart.

She leaves the room, and any hope I had of not crying is completely lost. I'm bawling in my hands, the emotions shredding me over a past I so desperately wish I could change.

Despite that, for once, it seems like the stars are aligning and everything is going my way. So why do I have a bad feeling gnawing in the pit of my stomach?

Ragnar

Narah's crying, and it fucking guts me to see her this way. A nerve twitches under my eye at the heaviness sinking deep within me, just like it had earlier when she threatened to leave. Fuck! I'm not strong enough for my heart to bear such a loss. Not again.

I'd lost my fated mate, and I was never meant to find anyone else to replace her. Then Narah broke into my life and destroyed everything. She's all I think about. All my wolf craves.

But sharing her? It shouldn't leave me vulnerable.

I need to be careful, I keep telling myself. It does no fucking good, though, because I've fallen head over heels for her. My wolf isn't helping here, either.

Images from my past rise of my fated mate...

"Ragnar, this isn't going to work," Eisa says, holding her chin up bravely. Her eyes are red like she's been crying, and even her quivering chin shows me how much she's struggling.

"What are you talking about?" I growl, but even that comes out croaky as my chest is cleaving in half. I grab her arm, but she wrenches it free and recoils from me like I'm a beast she fears.

"It's over, okay. Don't make this harder than it is. I don't love you. I tried, I really did, but..." She lowers her head, strawberry blonde hair tumbles over her face as she heaves for breath.

"But what?" I snarl. "It's Ven, isn't it? I've seen you two spending more time together, and I assumed you were friends... except I was a fucking idiot, wasn't I?"

"Ragnar, please don't..."

"Don't what?" Rage roars through me. I march up to her and rip the bag out of her hand, and toss it across the room. I grab her arm and haul her to my side.

"You want to hurt me?" she pulls against my hold. "Go ahead if it'll make you feel better. But it won't change my decision."

I blink at her but don't release her. "Have you forgotten we're fated mates, that if we part, your wolf will pant for mine for eternity? I gave you everything..."

She shakes her head, tears squeezing out from the corners of her eyes. "I-I know how to mask the pain," she stutters, ripping out of my grasp. "I'm sorry, but I can't do this. I love someone else."

I'm shaking, the room tilting around me.

I'm roaring on the inside while my fists clench, knuckles turning white. Fury fills me, controls me, drowns me in the darkest pits of my mind.

"Where the fuck is Ven?" I growl, storming out of the room.

Eisa's behind me, grabbing my shirt and pulling me backward. "Ragnar, no, please don't."

I shove her off me, and she stumbles back into the wall of the hallway. I see nothing but rage simmering so close to the surface.

I'm going to murder Ven.

Nothing hurts more than watching Eisa love another man.

I shake the past from my mind, studying Narah, hugging her knees to her chest. How does she expect me to share her? I've been patient this entire time, knowing my men flirt with her, but I had no clue she'd developed feelings for them. That pit of darkness swells inside me once more at the thought that I'm not her only one.

I remain rooted in the doorway to my room, wanting to encase this woman in my arms, to keep her all for myself, to call her mine, mine, mine. Swallowing the thickness in my throat, all I can think about is someone else fucking her, and it burns me alive.

Tensing, I clench my fists.

I don't hate my men—I never could—so now I'm left in an impossible situation. Is it all that different from what I'd heard Narah's mother tell her about choosing to sacrifice their father to protect his daughters?

Is that going to be me? Lose her, or learn to accept she will never be completely just mine?

Narah slides her feet underneath her ass on the couch, curling in on herself. She's so small, so fragile, yet unimaginable magic fills her veins.

I step into the room, and she looks up, quickly wiping her tears at my approach.

She doesn't say anything at first, but unspoken words hang in the air between us. Our earlier argument is a thorn in my side. Except, I'm not here to talk about that. Not now, at least.

"Are you okay?" I sit down beside her, elbows resting on my thighs, and glance over my shoulder at her.

She stares at the empty doorway, then at me. "Guess you heard everything?"

"I did."

"Believe it or not, some of these are happy tears." She gives me a wonky smile and wipes at her eyes. "I found my mother. Yay." A tear escapes her eye, and I catch it as it drips off the edge of her jaw.

"Family is fucking complicated," I say to her. She's absolutely beautiful, even with her red-rimmed eyes, her pink cheeks and nose. The ache of losing her is going to ruin me.

She makes a strange huffing sound. "Just when I thought my life wasn't horrible enough, and I was sure it couldn't get worse."

"Your mother made an impossible decision. While you can't change the past, you can celebrate what you do have now."

She inhales sharply and licks her dry lips, then looks at me with bravery in her amber eyes. "How do you begin to forgive someone you know got your father killed on purpose?"

Ghostly memories curl under my breastbone and squeeze, leaving me numb all over. My past has devastated me, and I haven't yet worked out how to make amends with it, so who am I to give advice? "I wish I could give you words of wisdom or something comforting, but maybe try forgetting how you feel and focus on what you deserve."

I'm not sure she believes me, with the narrow gaze aimed my way. That's her decision. We all have demons to live with, monsters who destroy us. And she has to decide if she'll run with her demons or let them consume her.

19

NARAH

Night seeps into the woodland around us, fraying at the edges of a large pond. We're in the middle of the woods behind the Wolf Mountains village, and overhead a billion stars explode across the heavens, glinting through the gaps of the canopy. I've always found nighttime beautiful, but tonight I'm jittery and keep fiddling with my hair or clothes.

The four Alphas take their place on either side of me, staring ahead at the water. Only a few words have been exchanged between us on the way to meet my mother, the tension between Ragnar and his men twisting my anxiety into knots.

I blame myself, and while the conversation between Ragnar and I had to happen, I'm not so sure this was the best timing because look at us now. We're about to remove a curse that might signal to the witches we've broken their spell. They might hurt Kaira, or they might declare war and come for us. Who the hell knows? Yet, Mother promises me she'll mask the detection somehow, but what if it doesn't work? Magic is fickle at best.

This is why I need my head screwed on without distraction.

"Okay, so what do we need to do?" Ragnar asks my mother in a gruff voice.

I twist around to where she stands behind us with one hand holding a blade, and another a bag of what she called herbs. She's in a scarlet robe, which I assume is for theatrics, but with the knife glinting in the moonlight, I'm having flashbacks to Lyssa cutting my hand. Sure, it healed fast thanks to my wolf, but I'm not a fan of being randomly cut again.

Shadows thread around us amid the lofty trees, animals call in the night, a howl sings in the distance, and owls hoot. There are so many sounds.

"Take your clothes off," Mother says softly.

I blink at her, not completely comfortable with this, but it doesn't seem to be bothering the men, who are ripping their gear off, and in seconds are butt naked, now all facing her. They stand proud with everything on display. Mother doesn't even look at them, but she opens the bag of herbs.

"Take a pinch and place it under your tongue."

"You need help undressing?" Crius leans down to my ear to ask.

I smirk, knowing it's exactly what he'd like, but I shake my head, wanting to just get this over with. I strip down, the cold against my skin covering me in goose-bumps. I can't help but wrap an arm across my chest.

Mother's in front of me, smiling, as I stick my other hand into the pouch.

"Are you sure this is going to work?"

"Trust me. I've removed hundreds of witch curses." She's so confident that I take the herbs and place them in my mouth. They are gritty under my tongue and taste like peppermint.

Mother drops the bag to the ground, pulls her sleeve up to her elbow, and without hesitation swipes the blade across her forearm.

I hiss, knowing the biting pain all too well, while she just smiles like it is nothing.

She moves in front of Crius first and dabs two fingers into her blood, then runs it across his forehead, down his nose, mouth, chin, and onto his chest.

"Enter the sacred water."

Crius twists and howls as he hurls himself into the water, headfirst, the splash striking the back of my legs. I roll my eyes. She sends the rest of the men into the water in the same manner before returning to me.

She marks me; and the blood is warm against my skin. "I can't tell you how happy I am to have you back in my life. There is so much I need to teach you and show you." The corners of her eyes crinkle deeply.

The urge to mention that she should have looked for us earlier lingers. But, like Ragnar suggested, I focus on what I deserve, not the bitterness that refuses to leave my gut over Father. Mother's help will ensure we're free of a curse, and she can help us get Kaira back.

In my head, it sounds too easy because nothing ever goes well for me, so I have to believe this will work.

Her eyes glisten as she takes my hand with her blood-stained one and leans in, whispering. "Narah. Are you sure you can trust these wolves you're with?"

I stiffen, and a sliver of panic claws at my chest at her unexpected words. "What do you mean?" I glance back at the men swimming around in the water, chatting quietly, though Ragnar is keeping to himself.

"They look really familiar to me, and not in a good way," she continues softly. "My mind's just not as good as it once was, and things are not so easy to recall these days. But I'm not getting good vibes from them."

"They've protected me until now," I whisper.

"I'm just saying to be careful, Narah. Something is not right with their energies."

Her warning bends in my mind, and a shiver snakes up my spine. After everything I've been through with these wolves, with the way I am drawn to them, this is the last thing I need to hear.

"Quickly now, get into the water." She nudges at my shoulder to get moving like she hadn't just dumped a bombshell on me.

I step carefully into the cold water, the ground pebbly and sharp under my feet.

Yet my stomach hurts worse from her words, and I wish she hadn't said anything in the first place.

I slosh through the water, going deeper. When I glance up, the men have gone quiet and are watching me carefully. I move faster and dunk under the cold embrace of the pond.

I meet Ragnar's gaze instantly. He's several feet away, and looking at him now leaves me torn. Part of me wants to swim over to him, another part is drawn to the other men, while my head reminds me of our unfinished argument. And now there's the warning Mother put into my head too. After this, she has to tell me what it means before it makes me go mad.

We're all just bobbing heads in the pond at midnight, treading water, and I face Mother. "It's really cold in here. Can we get started?"

"Yep, my balls are shriveling back into my body," Crius barks.

Mother steps into the water with feet bare and pauses. She murmurs something under her breath and claps once. The sound echoes in the woods around us, and silence falls over us.

My skin ripples as I wait.

Stone is suddenly sucked underwater, then Nikos.

I frantically splash to get to them, a small cry escaping my lips.

Ragnar rushes toward me, wild fear in his eyes, when he's also claimed. Wrenched under so fast, he's gone and only bubbles float to the surface.

"Mother, what are you doing?" I cry out, my words ragged.

I turn to Crius frantically, water sloshing around me, when something suddenly grabs my ankles.

I'm yanked underneath.

Terror grips me, my heart thundering against my ribcage.

I flail my arms wildly. It's too dark in the water, too murky to even make out my hand out in front of my face.

I battle to release my legs from whatever holds them. My lungs burn for oxygen, and I'm kicking crazily to free myself. I reach down desperately, finding vines bound around my ankles. They're so thick, so tight. I claw at them, but there's no way to tear them off.

Terror floods through me. Death is all I can think about. The terrifying notion that perhaps my mother lied to me... that I walked right into her trap. That we'll all die out in this pond and no one will ever know. Kaira will die with the witches, and Jae... she'll wait for me to never return.

Liar... please don't let my mother be a liar.

Pressure builds inside me, the ache in my chest, my head is close to bursting.

I can't hold on.

Magic gushes out of my body so fast that it rattles me. But at the same time, the sting of suffocating is too much. Too fucking much.

My mouth gapes open to desperately suck in air out of instinct. Water rushes inside, and my mind blackens in seconds.

Next thing I know, I'm kneeling on the bank of the river, coughing my lungs out.

It hurts so much that I'm crying from the agony. Crius lands in a heap right next to me, as if he's been scooped out of the pond and dumped there. Like me, he's coughing and throwing up water. Ragnar, Nikos, and Stone are the same. We've all been yanked out by magic, choking on the water in our lungs.

Every inch of me is exhausted like I've been walking for a week straight. If I closed my eyes now, I'd fall asleep.

I lift my head to my mother, who's farther from us now in the woods, maybe twenty feet, closing the cloak around her. She has a small lantern by her feet, and yet something looks different about her. Maybe it's the shadows?

"What did you do to us?" My arms tremble, I'm barely able to hold myself up.

"I removed your curse, Narah. Just as you asked me. And you know there is really only one way to eradicate someone else's curse." She pushes her dark hair off her face, and that's when I see her clearly. Where there were once wrinkles on her neck, now her skin is smooth and firm looking, her lips full, the creases from her eyes gone. She's younger, just as I remember her as a child.

What the hell?

I push myself up on shaky legs, unease curling in the pit of my stomach. "What does that mean?" I repeat louder as the men rise up beside me.

"It's not a big deal, sweetie. After a day of rest, you'll be back to normal. But each one of you is now curse free, so you're welcome."

"What the fuck! Answer Narah's damn question straight!" Ragnar growls, his chest puffed out.

She makes a huffing sound, her upper lip curling up and over a perfect line of white teeth. "Fine. You had to die for the curse to be removed. Then I brought you back to life. It's not a big issue. There is a very small chance you will experience side effects, but it's unlikely they will happen."

"The fuck! Side effects?" Crius bellows. "You've made us into zombies?"

Mother chuckles loudly. "Don't be ridiculous. I brought you back to life with your soul intact."

Fear replaces my earlier hope that things will finally go well. "H-how... Oh, shit. How can you say that's not a big issue? You didn't even tell us you were going to kill us."

Bile rises into my mouth like I'm going to be sick.

She bends over and lifts the lantern. "Would you have agreed to the ritual if I had? Come into the house when you've dried and dressed, then I'll explain everything. I've left some towels on the ground here." She glances down by her feet, then starts strolling down the path back toward the village, her lantern swinging in her hand.

"Fuck that," Stone snarls, studying his body like something might be missing.

Crius is checking out his cock, as if that somehow had been affected, while Nikos is heaving for breath, his face red with fury.

"She had no right," Stone snaps. "I've heard too many horror stories of what happens to people who come back from the dead. Fuck!"

I can't even defend my mother when I'm shaking with anger, trying to make sense of what she just did to us.

"Did you see how much younger she looked?" Ragnar asks. "She fed on us."

I chew on my lower lip, shaking violently, my teeth chattering. *Goddess, what has my mother done?*

"And I hate being played!" he roars.

I stare at the dark path Mother took, shaking my head. "But she wouldn't. She's helping us." I'm hugging myself tighter when Crius hands me a towel to dry off.

"Open your eyes, Narah," Ragnar growls. "She used us. How do we know for certain the curse has even been removed?"

I swallow hard, then clench my fists, stilling the tremble. "I'm going to find out the truth." Fury has me hurrying to collect my clothes and I dress quickly, even if I'm still soaking wet, and it's almost impossible to pull on my pants this way. But my pulse is a war drum.

I run after her, not bothering to wait for the men. I have to know the truth if it kills me.

A howl slices through the night air, then again, closer this time. It comes from behind me, and I can only imagine it's one of the men... or maybe a local. I don't care. I'm sprinting past the trees and ducking under low-hanging branches.

A blood-curdling scream pierces the air from up ahead.

My stomach drops as I imagine Mother falling over or something.

I sprint madly, my heart beating in my throat as a cacophony of shouts and growls erupts farther behind me. It's loud and terrifying. What the hell's going on? Are there men fighting?

But I won't stop... I can't.

Around the next bend, I come to a sudden, gut-wrenching stop.

Two black wolves are in my path, tearing into someone who's sprawled on the ground. The savage sounds of tearing, slurping, growling fill the air.

Then I catch a glimpse of her face beneath the beasts.

My knees weaken.

"Mamma!" I scream.

Magic catapults from my hands in seconds, jutting outward, striking the animals in the sides, throwing them off my mother in an explosive flash.

I sprint to her side, my knees scraping the dirt as I land on them. She's on her back, her chest and throat completely torn out, blood gushing. And her eyes wide open.

I cry out, my heart shattering like glass. I grip her arm, and every inch of me has gone icy cold with dread. It brings back horrible memories of burying my father, and I can't do this again. Not again.

"Please wake up. I can heal you. Anything, just don't die on me."

Without warning, strong hands grab me by the hair and wrench me backward.

I scream and fall back on my ass.

I snap my head up and am staring at the face of the monster who tried to kill me. Terror smothers me.

Martell!

His face twists into hatred. "See you very soon, Narah." His fist flies at my face and strikes hard.

Darkness claims me instantly.

CURSE OF THE FAE

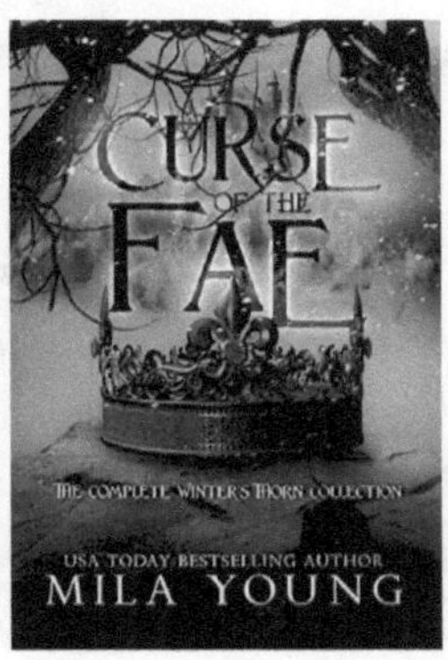

"She is breathtaking, powerful, everything we've been searching for. And once we convince her that she is ours, we will satisfy her in every way until her true potential is realized."

I am nothing. A girl with no past.

But then they crash into my world.

Three sexy-as-hell fae princes who insist I belong to them, that only they can satisfy my every need.

I want to reject them, but I can't deny the way my body reacts to theirs. I crave their touch, their lips against my skin, and the way they make me feel that I am so much more.

But when they take me to a magical realm where war brews like poison and once-powerful royals are slaughtered, I fear I've made a grave mistake.

My fae princes insist I'm important. I'm the key to saving them.

I want to believe them but these three three fae princes who have sworn to protect me are keeping dangerous secrets. Ones that if I don't unravel soon just might be the death of me...

Readers LOVE this enemies to lovers fae romance fantasy series with over 900 pages! Four books that include a strong heroine and three fae princes who will do anything to protect their fated mate. Lose yourself in this steamy paranormal romance with high action, suspense, forbidden attraction, and burning love scenes that will have you begging for more!

Curse of the Fae is a complete series and includes 4 full length books.

To Catch A Fae

To Seduce A Fae

To Tame A Fae

To Claim A Fae

A FREE STORY JUST FOR YOU ....

Did you enjoy Savage Sector and want more? Sign up for my newsletter at www.subscribepage.com/milayoung and you will receive a free novella from me as a thank you gift your joining my newsletter.

In addition, you'll be given special access to deleted and bonus scenes, new release announcements and so much more!

BOOKS BY MILA YOUNG

www.milayoungbooks.com

Shadowlands

Shadowlands Sector, One

Shadowlands Sector, Two

Shadowlands Sector, Three

Chosen Vampire Slayer

Night Kissed

Moon Kissed

Blood Kissed

The Alpha-Hole Duet

Real Alphas Bite

Kingdom of Wolves

Wild Moon

Wild Heart

Wild Girl

Wild Love

Winter's Thorn

<u>To Seduce A Fae</u>

<u>To Tame A Fae</u>

<u>To Claim A Fae</u>

Shadow Hunters Series

Boxed Set 1

Wicked Heat Series

Wicked Heat #1

Wicked Heat #2

Wicked Heat #3

Elemental Series

Taking Breath #1

Taking Breath #2

Gods and Monsters

Apollo Is Mine

Poseidon Is Mine

Ares Is Mine

Hades Is Mine

Sin Demons Co-write with Harper A. Brooks

Playing With Hellfire

Hell In A Handbasket

All Shot To Hell

To Hell And Back

When Hell Freezes Over

Hell On Earth

Haven Realm Series

Hunted (Little Red Riding Hood Retelling)

Cursed (Beauty and the Beast Retelling)

Entangled (Rapunzel Retelling)

Princess of Frost (Snow Queen)

Thief of Hearts Series Co-write with C.R. Jane

Siren Condemned

Siren Sacrificed

Siren Awakened

Broken Souls Series Co-write with C.R. Jane

School of Broken Souls

School of Broken Hearts

School of Broken Dreams

School of Broken Wings

Fallen World Series Co-write with C.R. Jane

Bound

Broken

Betrayed

Belong

Beautiful Beasts Academy

Manicures and Mayhem

Diamonds and Demons

Hexes and Hounds

Secrets and Shadows

Passions and Protectors

Ancients and Anarchy

Subscribe to Mila Young's Newsletter to receive exclusive content, latest updates, and giveaways. Join here.

ABOUT MILA YOUNG

**Find all Mila young books at
www.milayoungbooks.com**

Best-selling author, Mila Young tackles everything with the zeal and bravado of the fairytale heroes she grew up reading about. She slays monsters, real and imaginary, like there's no tomorrow. By day she rocks a keyboard as a marketing extraordinaire. At night she battles with her mighty pen-sword, creating fairytale retellings, and sexy ever after tales. In her spare time, she loves pretending she's a mighty warrior, walks on the beach with her dogs, cuddling up with her cats, and devouring every fantasy tale she can get her pinkies on.

Ready to read more and more from Mila Young?
www.subscribepage.com/milayoung

Join Mila's **Wicked Readers group** for exclusive content, latest news, and giveaway.

www.facebook.com/
groups/milayoungwickedreaders

For more information...
milayoungauthor@gmail.com

www.ingramcontent.com/pod-product-compliance
Lightning Source LLC
Chambersburg PA
CBHW050751190726
48285CB00005B/1616